Three Cavaliers

a novel

Tom Walsh

Living Life Fully Publications, U.S.A.

Published by Living Life Fully Publications
United States of America
http://www.livinglifefully.com

Three Cavaliers

ISBN: 978-0-6151-4402-3

Printed in the United States of America.

Living Life Fully Publications is a trademark of livinglifefully.com.

To Roswitha—

you being who you are
has helped me to grow
into being who I am.
Thank you.

Night was Jason's ally, the friend he needed to keep him company. It didn't ask any questions, and it let him be just who he was no matter what kind of shape he was in. No matter how pissed off he was, no matter how much of a failure he felt himself to be, no matter how useless he felt, no matter how little hope he allowed to pierce his armor, the night let Jason be, and he appreciated that. Night was even better in his car on the Interstate, where there in the darkness he felt the safety and comfort of complete isolation, complete anonymity. And though he wouldn't have voiced it to anyone else except perhaps the closest of friends, he also liked the fact that the darkness and the isolation allowed him to brood, let him turn on the self-pity and the self-righteous anger that he knew wasn't justified, but which made him feel just a little bit better by making him feel so awful.

The dim light from the car's instrument panel and the passing lights of the cars carrying their drivers and passengers to their destinations somewhere else gave him little comfort—it was the darkness that made him feel that even if nothing could go right, he still could find some solace in the complete lack of light that surrounded him as he drove through the night.

It surprised him sometimes just how rarely he got tired when he drove at night. It was almost two in the morning, and though he had been on the road some nine hours he felt just as alert as he had felt when he left Concord the previous afternoon.

Stopping for gas was the main pain in the ass that night. If he stopped he knew he'd have to see other people, and he simply wasn't in the mood to do that. Fortunately he didn't have to spend any time with them—his guess was that the last thing the attendants at the all-night gas stations wanted was to have some sort of in depth tête-à-tête with some stranger whose name they never would know. Besides, what could some stranger's opinions possibly add to his life, and what good could his thoughts bring to the life of someone who was making minimum wage to spend all night at some sterile convenience store-slash-gas station? He hated shallow small talk, and he especially hated it when he was in a mood as dark as the one he was feeling now. And how deep could anyone get in three and a half minutes of talk?

As unpleasant as it felt to him, his gas gauge left him with little choice—pull off at the next 24-hour station or risk an even longer encounter with someone driving a tow truck and bringing him gas on the auto club's dime. Ahead in the distance the glow of a huge Mobil sign violated the night with its overpowering presence, and Jason sighed. In a few minutes he hit his turn signal as he prepared to leave the highway. There was no one in his rear-view mirror who could benefit from the blinking light, but the force of habit was strong. He pulled into the new lane of the exit and downshifted to fourth, feeling the power of the engine as it revved up, almost doubling its rpm's. He felt the engine but he could hardly hear it above the music that he had cranked in the small compartment that had been his reality for the past nine hours.

He shifted down to third while he was still going faster than he should have been, and the car lurched awkwardly and slowed quickly; he pushed in the clutch again to let the car glide—the off ramp took him up a gentle incline, and he felt the gravity working to rob the car of its inertia, to cause it to come almost to a stop some twenty feet short of the stop sign. He laughed, but without any humor. He threw the car into first and let the clutch out quickly and the car jumped forward to cover the rest of the distance to the red-and-white octagon.

Jason didn't care where he was. He had no interest at all in knowing the name of the town he was in because he didn't give the slightest damn about it. He was pretty sure that he was still in Pennsylvania, but he wouldn't have bet any money on it. He knew where he was going, and he knew that Seattle was still a hell of a lot of miles away. He knew what he was leaving, and that it was a good nine hours behind him. It might as well have been twenty years behind him, for all that he felt about it—or didn't feel. All he had to do right now was fill the tank up with gas to get him a little bit further and buy himself a cup of coffee that might or might not help to keep him awake and keep him from running off the road and killing himself. He'd take the opportunity to get rid of the coffee from the last stop he had made, too.

If it weren't for the coffee and the need to use the urinal, he wouldn't have had to see a single person. He could have just slid his credit card through the slot at the pump, pushed a button to choose his grade of gas, and filled his tank without having to say a single word to a single person. Then like magic a statement would arrive in the mail weeks later telling him where he had spent his money that night, and then he'd finally actually have to pay for the gas. He liked the idea of not having to turn over any actual money when he bought stuff, but he hated the statements that reminded him how much he owed to the bank that had sent him the card.

He pulled up to the pump that was furthest away from the store and got out of the car, wincing as he used his feet and legs again for something other than pushing pedals on the floorboard, and taking a few slow, stiff steps to remind his leg muscles what walking was all about.

It was quiet at that time of night, save for the sound of crickets and whatever other insects were out in the woods outside of the pool of light that defined the gas station. He wondered if the insects were confused by the light, not knowing that it was so deep into the night that they should be asleep already. To them it probably always was daytime, or maybe even dusk on the other side of the trees that surrounded the lot. There were enough lights on to illuminate several homes, he was sure, and he figured that the bugs there never had the chance to know what real darkness was.

He glanced into the store and saw a tall middle-aged man peering out in his direction. He removed his car's gas cap and put the nozzle in and started filling his tank. Someone had removed the little attachment that would have allowed him to let go of the handle and let it shut itself off automatically, so he couldn't clean the smashed bodies of the bugs off his windshield until after he finished pumping the gas.

"Bastards," he muttered when he noticed it. There wasn't much more to say about the matter, though, so he just shook his head and looked out into the night, out towards the highway he had just come from, back towards the pavement that he knew stretched from the east coast all the way to the west coast without end. And he was going to ride that pavement almost as far west as he could.

When he finished with the gas he replaced the cap and cleaned his windshield. He had to scrape hard to get rid of some of the remains of insects that had lost their lives by smashing against the glass, innocent victims of human technology, and Jason felt a bit sorry for them. They never would have had any idea what hit them, he found himself thinking. But maybe that's the best way to go—quickly and completely, hit so hard that you become nothing more than a dull yellow splotch because your insides are now on the outside. It would sure as hell be better than dying slowly and painfully, anyway.

He made his way slowly into the store, heading first for the bathroom. The guy behind the counter didn't even look up as Jason entered the store, and Jason was glad of that. It kept alive his illusion of solitude.

He felt fortunate that he didn't have to spend much time in the bathroom or sit down. It wasn't the cleanest place in the world, and the smell would have made him sick if he had had to bear it long. But in just a couple of minutes he was back out in the store, looking for the coffee. It wasn't hard to find, as the stores at gas stations all were becoming more and more similar and devoting more and more space to coffee. It was obviously one of the best selling products that they could offer to travelers in the middle of the night, since so many people considered coffee to be the main thing that kept them alive in the middle of the night.

He glanced over at the guy behind the cash register. He didn't envy him his job. All alone in the middle of the night with nothing else around, the guy seemed pretty vulnerable. He looked tough enough, some six-feet-two and stocky as hell, but how tough can you be when there's no one around to back you up? He wouldn't want to deal with that kind of stress every night, wondering who would be the next customer to walk in and what he'd want. He especially wouldn't want it when he was in his fifties, like this guy was. He would hate to think of himself reaching that age and still having to work a graveyard shift just to make ends meet. What other reason could there be to work such a shift? Or maybe the guy worked there to get away from his wife—who knew?

He finished making his coffee and put on one of the plastic covers with the little hole for drinking through, and he grabbed a muffin from a basket next to the coffee pots and then stopped and looked around to see if there might be something else there that he wanted or needed. He didn't see anything. He picked up his coffee and took it to the register.

"Good morning," the cashier said as he approached.

"Howdy," Jason said, putting down the coffee and muffin and reaching in his pocket for his money.

"That be it?" Jason guessed that the cashier was some sort of retired military—he just had that look about him. His nametag said that his name was Fred. That was more than Jason really wanted to know right then—he preferred complete anonymity. He didn't want to know any names. He didn't even want to be thinking that this Fred guy probably had a wife at home and maybe even a kid or two living who-knows-where. He didn't want to know anything about anyone else for a while, not until he had a chance to figure his own life out, and God knew how long that was going to take. "Two seventy-three," Fred said after he punched a few buttons on the register. His voice was surprisingly gentle. He saw the five in Jason's hand and had the change ready before he even took the money; he handed Jason two ones, a quarter and a couple of pennies with his left hand as he took the five with his right.

"Thanks," Jason said quietly, and picked up the muffin and the cup.

"You're heading west, aren't you?" Fred asked, but it was more of a statement than a question.

Jason stopped, taken aback by his words. "Yeah, I am," he said, suddenly unsure of himself, knowing that something else had to be coming. "Why?"

"You know," Fred said quietly, "you could really help someone out tonight if you were up to it." Fred's eyes were the brightest and clearest blue eyes that Jason had ever seen, and right now they were fixed on Jason's eyes. Jason knew that he was looking into the eyes of a good person. How the hell he knew that, he had no idea. He just did. And it was something that he didn't want to know, because he was going to turn Fred down, no matter what. And it was harder turning down favors for people who were good people. But the last thing that Jason was in the mood for was to be a Good Samaritan.

"What are you talking about?" he asked, immediately regretting the question. He should have just said sorry and walked out, he knew.

Fred nodded his head in the direction of a small table in one corner of the store, where Jason noticed for the first time that he and Fred weren't alone in the store. An old man was sitting at the table, a very small old man. "That guy needs a ride, real bad," Fred said.

"Sorry," Jason said, shaking his head. "I just can't take the risk. You never know what's going to happen when you pick up hitchhikers."

"He's not a hitchhiker," Fred said simply. "And I can vouch for him. Ain't nothing gonna happen to you 'cause of him."

Jason shook his head again. "Look, man, I'm sorry, but I'm really not in the mood to have a passenger tonight. I've got a lot on my mind. He'd hate my company anyway."

Fred kept looking at him as if he were sparring with him, trying to figure out Jason's weaknesses as they spoke, trying to find just the right argument that would tear down his defenses and cause him to submit. That made Jason uncomfortable—he hated the idea of being figured out, of someone knowing him so well and discovering some side of him that even he didn't know existed.

"Look, the guy's harmless, and he really needs to get out west really soon. Something happened in his family that he won't tell me about, and he needs to go somewhere in Idaho. And since you're heading west. . . ." He raised his eyebrows like some kind of dad who was teaching his kid an important lesson and hoping the kid came up with the answer himself, a dad who knew that the kid already knew what to do, but who wanted him to say it.

"I'm heading west, but I'm heading west alone," Jason said, and he knew that with those words, he should start walking towards the door, leaving behind one more statement to close the conversation. He was dismayed to discover that his feet stayed planted on the floor below him. That couldn't be a good sign, he realized with a sinking feeling. "Besides," he added, "he wouldn't like my music. Too loud."

"Then I'll give him some toilet paper to stuff in his ears," Fred said, seemingly aware that he had gained an advantage. "No big deal. And he can ride in the back seat and never say a word the whole way. Just take him as far as you can take him."

"And take him off your hands."

Fred smiled. "He's no bother to me. Look at how quiet he is. I just feel bad for him. I'd like to think that if I ever got myself into a situation like his, someone would help me out. Where you headin'?"

"Seattle," Jason muttered, under his breath and against his better judgment. He didn't want to tell Fred a damned thing, and he was starting to resent Fred's ability to keep him engaged in a conversation that he didn't want to be involved in. He was wishing that he had waited one more exit to get gas.

"Then that's perfect!" Fred said enthusiastically. "You'll be going through Idaho, and you can drop him off on the way. And if you get to the point where you can't stand him before Idaho, you can drop him off at a bus station somewhere. You get someone to help keep you awake while you drive, and I don't have to kick some poor old guy out of my store."

Jason knew that the deal was done, even though he hadn't agreed to anything. There was even a part inside of him that even told him that he was doing the right thing, the kind thing, the compassionate thing. That part of himself pissed off the rest of him. He wanted to get out to his car and take off and never think of the store or Fred or the old man again, but now there was unfinished business that Fred had thrust upon him. He suddenly had a decision to make, and only then could he get going.

He wanted to tell Fred to shove it, to tell him that he hadn't had any right to put Jason in such a position. He wanted to say no and walk out the door, but that same weak part of himself knew that wasn't the right thing to do. He had been enjoying—in a sick sort of way—feeling sorry for himself, and with someone else in the car his self-pity was bound to be much less satisfying. He wouldn't be able to feel as good about feeling bad any more.

He looked over at the old man, who was sitting quietly at the table eating a candy bar and drinking a cup of coffee. He hadn't even looked over at them, and Jason wondered if he were hard of hearing or just polite enough not to want to pressure him into giving him a ride.

He could think of tons of reasons why it would be a bad idea to take the guy. He probably smelled bad, or he smoked. He could have been one of those old guys who talked on and on, saying the same things over and over again like his stories were something new without ever noticing that the other person had no interest at all in what he was talking about. He might have been some sort of whack job who was going to talk crazy shit all night long. Maybe he was just going to fall asleep as soon as he got into the car and pass gas for hours, forcing Jason to drive with the windows open at 70 miles an hour. Or else he talked super slow and would want to talk all the time, taking forever to finish his sentences and driving Jason up a wall.

"Maybe," Fred said quietly, somehow reading his mind, "he's just some nice guy who really needs someone's help— help that you're in a perfect position to give him."

"Shit!" Jason muttered. "All right, I'll take him. But he just rides along with me. I don't have to be friends with him or anything. I'm not in the mood for any more friends in my life right now."

Fred cocked his head questioningly, as if he had heard something interesting in Jason's words, but then he turned quickly towards the old man.

"Hey, Hector!" he called out, fairly loudly. "Come on over here—we've got you a ride."

The old man looked over at Fred with a look of disbelief on his face, then at Jason. His expression spoke of everything that Jason didn't want to see right then— gratitude and appreciation and even surprise. Jason didn't need for anyone to be grateful to him right then. Hector picked up his coffee cup, then he stood and made his way slowly over to the two men.

"You will take me out west?" he asked Jason carefully, as if he were afraid to say the wrong words and have Jason suddenly change his mind.

"I guess so," Jason muttered. Hector and Fred exchanged a glance that acknowledged Jason's reluctance, and that look pierced Jason's armor more than any words could have. He was doing the right thing, he was sure, but he had had to be talked into it and he still wasn't happy about it. He was the one who always told his friends that life always brings surprises and that they should embrace them and learn from them, and now here he was, wallowing so deeply in his own self-pity that he wasn't even able to do something so simple without making it seem like something wrong.

"If it is a problem for you," Hector said quietly and humbly, "then you need not give me a ride. I will understand. I can wait for someone else who is going in that direction."

"Just get whatever stuff you've got. I want to get on the road."

Hector glanced again at Fred, who nodded almost imperceptibly. He turned and went back to the table and grabbed a small blue duffel bag that had been lying on the chair opposite him.

If nothing else, Jason was relieved to note, at least he seemed to be a nice person. He didn't look like someone who was going to be a complete jerk and talk about his many conquests of women or the times he had kicked so-and-so's ass for looking at him the wrong way. Hector seemed to be pretty down-to-earth. He had to be in his late sixties, Jason guessed, and he didn't look like he was out to impress anyone. Jason couldn't tell if he was Mexican or South American, but he supposed it didn't matter—he was sure he would find out soon enough. Hector was the same height as Jason, some five feet ten, though he was a good ten pounds lighter than Jason's 170 pounds.

"Let's go," Jason said quietly when Hector came right back, trying not to sound like a jerk himself. "I need to get going."

Fred pushed himself up from where he had been leaning on the counter. "That's right good of you, man," he said. "The gas is on me."

"Thanks," Jason said wryly. "I paid for the gas at the pump with my credit card."

"Oh, yeah," Fred said, seeming surprised but unconcerned. "Guess it isn't on me then. I'll pick up the tab for the coffee and muffin, then."

"I already paid for the coffee and muffin."

"Right." Fred paused as if he were thinking about what else he might offer. Then he grinned. "Have a good trip, then."

Chapter 2

To Jason's great relief, Hector didn't smell bad. That was one point for him. When they reached his car, Hector motioned to the back seat. "I can sit in the back," he said quietly. "I will not bother you at all."

Jason wanted nothing more than to have the man put in some earplugs and crawl into the trunk so that he could crank his stereo and not have to worry if it bothered his new passenger, and he was in no mood to be a gracious host. Somehow, though, even when it went against his better judgment when his own self-gratification was dominant in his mind, he knew he had to treat Hector like a human being. The idea irked the hell out of him, but there it was.

"No, you don't have to do that," he said. "Sit in front. Don't worry about it."

"I am not worried about anything," Hector replied. "You are doing me a very great favor, and I appreciate it. I will do my best not to be a burden upon you. Idaho is very far away."

Jason sighed. Now there was a pleasant thought. "You're not a burden," he said, knowing that everything about himself for the last five minutes—his tone of voice, his attitude, the look that he knew he had in his eyes, his body language—had told Hector that he was, indeed, a burden, and that Jason was lying when he said he wasn't. Hector went to the passenger door and tried it, finding it locked. His movements were slow and relaxed, with no hurry or pressure that Jason could see. He didn't look at Jason when he found the door locked, as if he didn't want to give the impression that he expected something of him. He just kept his eyes looking down at the top of the car, and Jason found himself thinking that he wasn't sure if Hector's actions were submissive or humble. It didn't really matter, he knew. He got in the driver's side and unlocked the other door for Hector, who got in quickly and stowed his bag on the floor at his feet.

"You can put your bag in the back if you want," Jason told him. "Give you more room for your feet."

"Thank you," Hector replied. "I do not need too much room. At my age, I have stopped taking up as much space as I used to."

Jason glanced over at him. What the hell was that supposed to mean? He had a feeling that he should be smiling at a joke, but he wasn't sure. Hector was reaching for his seatbelt, so he didn't notice Jason glancing at him. Jason decided that he liked the idea, and he wondered how much space he took up himself.

"This is a very nice car," Hector said quietly as Jason started it up and they started moving. "What kind of car is it?"

"It's a Cavalier," Jason said. "Nothing fancy, but it gets me where I'm going with no problems."

"Cavalier," Hector repeated, almost to himself. "A good name. It means 'gentleman.' In Spanish, the word is *caballero*—it sounds very similar."

"I suppose it does," Jason replied, relieved that Hector at least seemed to be a nice person, and even more relieved now that they were in the car that he didn't smell bad.

The next ten minutes were quiet. Jason guided the car onto the highway and set the cruise control, then he turned the stereo on at a much lower volume than before. His mind was now on Hector and all that had happened at the gas station, and he made a mental note that if ever were to pass by there again he'd drop by and give Fred a piece of his mind. What the hell had it meant when Fred had said that he could vouch for Hector, anyway? Jason had no idea who Fred was, so what good did it do for him to vouch for someone else? Some things just made no sense, but it usually took Jason a while to figure it out when they didn't. He never had the good, quick comeback to anything that didn't make sense.

He half hoped that Hector would fall asleep and stay asleep all the way to Idaho, but since they were only somewhere in western Pennsylvania, that didn't seem very likely.

"Where are you from?" Jason asked aloud suddenly. Hector looked over at him quickly, as if he were surprised to hear Jason's voice.

"Originally," he answered, "I am from Guaymas, Mexico. It is a very beautiful port city. But I have lived many years in Pocatello, Idaho. I am going to see my son and his wife and my new granddaughter there. I have never seen her."

"That's really cool," Jason said quietly, not sure whether he should try to keep a conversation going or be satisfied that he had fulfilled the bare minimum of social courtesy by asking his passenger where he was from.

"Where are you from?" Hector asked, almost hesitantly, as if he weren't sure whether he should push his luck by asking any questions or not.

"I guess just New England," Jason said carelessly. "We moved a few times when I was a kid, so I grew up in a few different places. I can't call any of them home, really. They don't feel like home, anyway."

"That is too bad," Hector replied. "My life was very similar when I was a child. My parents were migrant farmers when I was very young, and we traveled always from farm to farm, from state to state, depending on the season, wherever there was work. We never stayed anywhere for more than a couple of months for many years."

"Wow—that must have been rough," Jason said. "How did you ever go to school?"

Hector shrugged almost unnoticeably. "Usually we did not. When we could, the teachers were very kind to us and they did their best to teach us what they could. It usually was not much in such a short time, but something was better than nothing. And when they were nice to us, it made us feel better about ourselves. But not everyone was nice to us, of course."

"I can imagine," Jason mused. "People can be real sons of bitches when you're not like them, can't they?"

Hector glanced over at Jason, then thought for several moments before replying. "I no longer think of them as sons of bitches," he said. "I now think of them as very sad people who probably never have known what it means truly to be a human being. They probably will never know what love truly is, and they probably never will know the meaning of peace. I cannot imagine dying without having experienced peace. I am grateful that in my life I have learned what the word means and how to live it. I was not always so, though. I used to hate with a great deal of passion, and I let that hatred hurt me for several years. I could have used all of that passion to accomplish good things, but instead I used it to express only anger." He paused. "But I am sure that you do not want to hear an old man ramble on about his past here in the middle of the night in Pennsylvania."

Jason laughed. "What the hell else is there to do in the middle of the night on an Interstate in Pennsylvania?"

Hector looked over at him, and for the first time in the car they made eye contact, even if they couldn't clearly see each other's eyes in the dim glow of the instrument panel. Jason was suddenly aware that he was glad that the old man was there with him. He didn't know why and it didn't make any sense to him, but it was so. He did know that for at least half an hour now he hadn't been focused on his problems, and that was actually a relief. He felt all of a sudden that he had known Hector for a very long time, that this was no stranger sitting there next to him.

Hector looked through the windshield, obviously deep in thought. Jason gave him time to gather his thoughts, and he even reached out and turned down the volume on the radio. He felt tension flowing out of him as he finally accepted the man's presence and stopped fighting it. He knew that in doing so, he was simply being the person he usually was, not the pissed-off jerk who was so unwilling to give up his precious privacy. No matter how strong the reasons for his anger, he knew that the privacy would have served no purpose but to help him stay angry, help him remain in his dark mood. And even though he loved the dark mood while he was in it, he always regarded it with fear and loathing when it would finally pass.

"I wasn't always angry," Hector said. "When I was a child, I was a very happy child. I liked people. I liked being with them and talking to them and listening to them and doing things with them. I liked everyone, even the ones that other people didn't like. And I liked being that way. Even though we moved from place to place, I always found friends and I always had people to be with."

Jason settled into his seat, focused on the road, and listened to his guest's words. Suddenly, the darkness wasn't all about being alone and isolated. Now, the darkness was something else. Now it was comforting, even protective.

"My father was a very good man, a man who worked very hard all the time for his family. He worked so hard to support us, though, that he never was able to spend any time with us. He was in the fields from six in the morning until eight at night sometimes, and when he came home all he could do was eat his dinner and go to bed. Then he would be gone in the morning before we even woke up.

When I was younger, I admired him, but now I also feel sad, knowing the sacrifices that he made so we could eat and have clothes to wear to school. He never experienced the rewards of supporting a family, and we never felt what it was like to be close to our father.

"My mother did all she could for my sister and me. She made the food be enough, no matter how little we had, and she gave our father all the support and encouragement she could. I know now that she was a very lonely woman who wanted to be with her husband, but I never saw that, then. It is funny how much we think we know when we are very young, and how much we find out later that we did not know at all.

"She was a beautiful woman, I think, with a smile that took away all of my pain when I fell down and hurt my arm or when another child would tease me or mock me. But I think all children see their mothers as beautiful women, no matter what they look like. It is a part of us that is a great shame to lose as we grow older.

"The two of them had come to the United States from Guaymas when I was only five years old, and my sister was three. They came because they wanted to offer us a better life than we could find in Guaymas, to give us more possibilities as we grew older. I believe my father could have found other work that was more stable, but he actually loved the migrant work—he said that he would much rather spend the day in the sunshine working with the plants and the soil than to be locked up in a factory doing the same work over and over, never seeing daylight all the time he was there. His brother had found work in a slaughterhouse in Colorado, and he tried to get my father to come there and work with him. My father would not go. I believe that my mother wanted to go to Colorado so that my sister and I would not have to move any more, and would be able to go to school and make friends, but she knew of my father's love of the land and of growing things. That is something that I inherited from him—I also love growing things and working with the soil. They are a part of life that is very important to me.

"I was happy with the life, for I had never known anything else. It was my world, and it was very normal for me. When I would meet children at school who had never left their towns, who had even lived in the same houses their entire lives, I felt sad for them. They didn't know what it was like to move somewhere else and start all over again, to set up a new place to live that would be your home for just a very short time."

Hector paused, looking out the passenger window. Jason wanted to hear more.

"What was your mother's name?" he asked quietly.

"Maria," Hector replied. "Almost all women from Mexico were named Maria then. Ana Maria or Maria Dolores—it did not matter. Maria something. It is just the way things were. Ana Maria Agueda Sanchez Garcia. She had three first names, and she deserved to have three. She went by Maria, though. She was a splendid woman. My father was named Pedro Gutierrez Maldonado. They were very good people.

"Like I told you before, I was not always angry. Until I was sixteen years old, I was a very happy boy, even if I did not have a true home or good friends. I had my family and I had my faith in God and I had by then started to work myself, and I finally was able to spend time with my father, even if it was out in the fields. I could work only in the evenings and on weekends, for my parents insisted that I go to school, but that was enough for me. I was getting to know my father in ways that I had never known him before, and I could see how much better he did the work than the other people we worked with. It made me admire him even more to see this. A part of me that always had been empty was being filled up like an empty lake that had suffered through many years of drought in the desert.

"One day in July, in late July when we were up in Idaho working on a potato farm, my father lost his arm in the machine that tilled the earth. He was walking alongside it as someone else was driving it, and he tripped and fell. How he tripped, I never shall know, for it made no sense—he always was a very careful man. But he tripped and his arm got caught in the part that ripped open the earth, and he lost the arm. I am very glad that I was not there when it happened, for I don't know what it would have done to me to see my father hurt so badly.

"They took him to the hospital where they took off what was left of the arm, and we were left wondering how my father would be and how we would be able to survive without the money he earned. The second question was simple—obviously, I would take his place and begin to work full-time, which I did the next day. The first question became simple very soon, for my father developed an infection and died less than two weeks after the accident."

"Oh, wow," Jason said quietly. "I'm sorry to hear that. I can see why you'd be angry."

"I was very sorry, too," Hector replied, shrugging. "It was very sad for us, for my family. But my father's death was not the reason I was angry. That came very soon after he died, when the owner of the land we were working on sent us away. He paid us for my father's last week of work, and he paid me for my work, and he told us we were no longer welcome on his land. His foreman told us—he didn't have the courage or the respect to do so himself. We were shocked, for we could not understand why he would do such a thing to us. I understand now that he was afraid that he might have to pay us a lot of money for my father's death if we were to find out that we had legal rights, but at the time we had no idea that we had any rights at all. We just wanted to work and to make our livings. We were pushed off the farm while it was still too early to move further south, with nowhere else to go.

"I felt betrayed. My father had given his very life to this man and to his farm, yet my father's family was being pushed off the land and pushed out of work. I could not understand the lack of loyalty, the lack of compassion and humanity that this man was showing. I was confused and betrayed, and I started to become angry. I took it out on almost everyone that I met. My mother tried to calm me down, and for the next two years she spent more time trying to help me deal with my anger than she spent on herself. Perhaps the fact that she had to watch out for me helped her to block out much of her grief—I don't know.

"That was my first death."

Jason wasn't sure what Hector meant. It seemed obvious, but there was something in the way that Hector had had spoken the words that made the obvious explanation seem insufficient. "Do you mean that was the first death you experienced in your life?" Jason asked.

"No. I mean that it was the first time I died."

Jason thought it over for a moment. "That doesn't make any sense."

Hector looked over at Jason. "Perhaps not," he said simply. "But perhaps it does. I know that one day I was one person, but two weeks later I was a different person. The Hector Gutierrez Sanchez that I was one day no longer was there the next. I had all the same memories as that other person, and people who had known me before still recognized me as someone they knew, but I was not the same person. The person I had been had died."

"I guess if you want to see it that way. . . ."

"Tell me," Hector said respectfully, "are you exactly the same person you were five years ago? Two years ago?"

"No, not at all. I've learned things. I've grown. I've been developing as a person, I guess. But yes—I'm still the same person. I mean, I'm still in the same body and all."

"Perhaps you see it that way only because you wish to hold on to what you were. Because you are afraid to let it go. Perhaps you are frightened to let go of who you were because you are frightened of who you may become." Hector spoke matter-of-factly, with no hint of certainty that he was right, with no sign that he felt he was teaching Jason something. He was making no effort to convince Jason that he was right, and that threw Jason off. He didn't know how to respond. He was used to people telling him what they believed almost as if they wished to challenge him, and he was used to arguing his side, which he usually thought of almost immediately. Here, though, there was no challenge, no need for him to jump to defend his own beliefs. Rather, there almost seemed to be an invitation to think more deeply, to reflect upon the words that Hector had spoken and the thoughts they expressed.

It made Jason very uncomfortable.

"So you're saying that I'm carrying around the person I used to be because I'm afraid of what I might be?" he asked, almost defensively. His old habits were very strong.

"No, no, no, *mijo*—I am saying nothing like that. I am only telling you that on the day we were forced to leave the farm that killed my father, I died. My body lived on, but the person I was no longer lived. The new person used what my brain had known before for everything it needed—language and eating and knowing people—but I was not the same person. I was angry at the world when before I had felt no anger. I felt isolated and lonely and confused when before I had felt a part of things.

"My mother started working illegally in a factory in Pocatello where some friends had found her work, but it was very difficult work that took much from her. We moved into a very small apartment that really was just two rooms and a bathroom, and there we lived for the next three years. I was sixteen at the time and I wanted to work to earn money to help the family, but my mother would not let me go to work in the factory with her. She made me go to school because she said that she didn't want her children ever to face the same problems that she was facing.

"Our apartment was on the edge of the town, in a building that was very old. It was very hot in the summer and very cold in the winter, and I slept on an old couch that was left in the apartment when we moved in. My mother and my sister shared a mattress on the floor in the bedroom. There was also an old dresser that was missing two drawers, but that still had one drawer for each of us. Even with just one drawer, I never had enough clothes to fill it. I believe that caused my mother much shame. I went to school every day, but since we were not able to get green cards, we had to be very careful not to call attention to ourselves. I think the people of the town knew us, somehow, and knew that we were harmless. They never gave us any problems, not even the police. We were very lucky.

"I also was very lucky that I was the type of person who kept his anger inside. I was mad at the entire world for what had happened to my father and my family, but I took that anger out only on myself. I never was satisfied with myself or with anything that I did, and for a long time I had no friends at all. Who would want to be a friend with someone who wasn't able to be a friend? I used to blame the world also because I had no friends, but I saw later that I caused that myself. Most of us cause our own lives to happen the way they do, but we don't see it until it's far too late."

"Now that's something that I have to disagree with you on," Jason said. "Tons of people do all sorts of crap to us that change our lives in bad ways. You can't say that we cause everything in our lives to happen the way things do."

"But I can say that, no? Even if you do not agree with me?"

"Well, yeah—it's just an expression. You can say it, of course, but it can't be right. It just doesn't make any sense at all."

"Perhaps it does not make sense because you want to apply logic and find logical reasons for things that defy logic. One day, when you have as many years as I have, you will see that there are many limits to what logic can explain to us. After you have lived through a long life with many different experiences, it will be easier for you to believe me. Right now, you are very young, and there is still much in this world for you to experience, much for you to learn. And that is very good. While you are young, be young, and live life as a young person lives life. Do many new things, and take many chances. The lessons of your life will come to you when they are supposed to. But it is a mistake to believe that we understand all about life before we have experienced life for many, many years. Even then. . . ." his voice trailed off, and he paused for a moment. "Even now, after many, many years, there is still so much that I do not understand about life. But there is also much that I have learned, much that I can share before I die and move on."

"Yeah, well I figure I'll be lucky if I get in as many years as you have, Hector," Jason replied, feeling some of the negativity he had so recently felt creeping back into his mind. "We all aren't meant to live long lives, you know." He ignored that fact that Hector looked at him, puzzled, and they drove on in silence for several very long minutes. Then he heard Hector's breathing change, become very deep and very regular, and he knew that Hector had fallen asleep. They were only about an hour away from Ohio.

The night didn't feel as much like an ally as it had earlier. Jason didn't feel a need for an ally any more, didn't feel the need to be isolated and alone and protected by the darkness all around him. He listened to Hector breathe and he realized that giving him a ride was probably the best thing he could have done for himself. It was probably better for him than it was for Hector, keeping him from dwelling on all the crap that he suddenly didn't want to be dwelling on any longer.

Chapter Three

By the time they hit Ohio he could see in his rear-view mirror the first touches of light on the horizon behind him. He was looking forward to the morning—it had been a long time since he had last experienced a sunrise and the start of a new day. Besides, he was starving, and he knew that he'd need to stop and eat soon. He still wasn't tired, a fact that surprised him a bit, but he was glad of it and had long before decided to drive until he couldn't drive any longer.

There were a lot of things that Jason liked about being on the road, and eating was one of them. His mind was stuck on a plate of eggs and bacon and hash browns and toast, even though he normally didn't eat much of anything for breakfast. There was something pleasant about the feeling of walking into a restaurant that he had never seen before and would never see again, sitting down and ordering food from someone he'd never see again. It was something that he hadn't experienced for a very long time, since the last time he and Lance had taken a long road trip; the memories of the trip south suddenly washed over him like a hot summer wind, filling his mind with images of days gone by, things long ago seen and heard and felt.

He shook his head to clear it and refocused on the road. He rolled down his window to let the fresh air keep his concentration focused on the present moment, the present place. The rush of cool air into the car woke Hector, who had been leaning against the door and sleeping soundly. Now he stirred, looking about himself with a bit of confusion until he got his bearings and realized where he was.

"Good morning," Jason said, almost cheerfully. He was glad to have someone to talk to, someone to distract him from the memories he had been trying so hard to forget. "We're in Ohio."

"Good," Hector said quietly. "Ohio's good."

"I'm getting really hungry," Jason said. "I'm going to stop for breakfast in about ten miles, okay? I saw a sign for a restaurant that looks pretty good."

"Yes, of course—that's fine," Hector replied. "It will be good to be able to use the bathroom, also."

"Yes, it will. Are you hungry?"

Hector shrugged. "I don't know yet. I just woke up. It usually takes some time for my brain and my body to start working together. It's very strange. Once I fell asleep in my hammock in the back yard, and when I woke up it was raining. I lay there for several minutes before I realized that I needed to go inside. I was very wet."

Jason laughed. "I'm just the opposite—I get groggy before I fall asleep, and then nothing works with anything else. I'm completely useless."

"They say that every time we fall asleep, it is a small death."

"Who are 'they'?"

"People. It doesn't matter which ones. You have been driving all night? And you are not getting tired?"

"No, not at all. It's really weird—when I'm driving, I hardly ever get sleepy. I'll pull over to sleep for three or four hours this afternoon, and then I'm good to go for quite a while. I can do that for two or three days, usually. It's kind of cool."

"I would offer to drive, but I no longer have a license to do so. You do not think that it might be dangerous to continue driving?"

"No, not at all. If I thought there were any danger of me falling asleep, I'd just pull over. Hell, the last thing I want to do is die in a car wreck just because I was too stupid or stubborn to pull over and catch some shut-eye. There are better ways to die."

"Yes," Hector agreed. "Yes, there are."

"Speaking of dying, you never finished your story last night. You said that you died, but you never said what happened afterwards."

"Yes, I did tell you. I was angry."

Jason looked over at him in disbelief. "But that's not telling me anything, now is it? What does that mean? What did you do? What happened to you? You left me with more questions than answers, and everyone knows that's not fair."

"Who is everyone?"

Jason laughed. "People. It doesn't matter which ones."

Hector smiled. "And what is 'fair'?"

"You know—fair. It's like implying to someone that you're going to say something to them, and then not saying it. Like saying 'Wow!' really loud, and then when someone says 'What?' you say 'Oh, nothing.' It leaves me hanging. It's not fair."

"Perhaps I am finished with my story, and what you are asking for is another story entirely."

Jason thought that over. "I guess that could be. Are you going to tell me the other story, then?"

"I can tell you another story if you would like, but perhaps it would be better to tell you over breakfast. My body and my mind are working together now, but all they both want to do is go to the bathroom, not tell stories."

"Five more minutes and we'll be there. I hope you can hold out that long."

"So do I."

The exit they took led to an entire highway community—three gas stations, two fast-food restaurants, and a regular restaurant, all of which seemed to exist only for the people who were passing by in their cars on their ways to somewhere else. There were no homes and no other businesses.

"I hope the restaurant's open," Jason muttered. "I'm sure not in the mood for fast food." He pulled into the parking lot and assumed from the presence of five other cars that the restaurant was open. He parked the car and turned the key to kill the engine. It was always a strange sensation to turn off the engine on long trips. The car seemed to be so faithful, so willing to do the job it was created to perform, and it felt almost a shame to cut it off while it was still willing to do what it was supposed to do.

"You do have money, don't you?" he asked Hector. "Because if you don't, I can loan you some until we get to Pocatello."

Hector smiled. "I have money," he said. "But thank you."

"No problem," Jason said and got out of the car, feeling mild pain shoot through his legs as they bore his weight once more. They hadn't had much to do since he had left New Hampshire the previous evening, and they were protesting their lack of use even more than they had at the gas station earlier. Just wait until two days from now, Jason told himself. That's something to look forward to.

The restaurant was a cozy place—simple and comfortable. All of the decorations were in what Jason could only guess was Midwestern country style—there were lots of pigs and cows and other livestock in the paintings he saw, and there were small wood carvings of barnyard animals scattered about the dining room on the counter and tables. Jason had to smile. It was just the sort of thing that he and his friends back in Concord would have mocked, but it seemed to work quite well at five-thirty in the morning in a small homey restaurant in Ohio.

"Just the two of you?" the waitress asked, pulling a pair of menus from underneath the greeter's pedestal near the door. Her name was Jenny, according to the name tag on her apron.

"Yep," Jason replied. "Just us."

"I hope non-smoking's okay," she said with a laugh, "because the whole place is non-smoking." She started away, and Jason and Hector followed her.

"Non-smoking's fine, then," Jason said for no real reason as she led them to booth next to the picture window that looked out onto the parking lot. "Oh, good," Jason said as he slid into his seat. "Now I get to look at my car from the outside."

Jenny laughed. "Sorry, but it's the best view we've got. Actually, it's the only view we've got. Can I get you some coffee?" Both Jason and Hector said yes, so she left menus with them and went to get the coffee.

Hector was regarding Jason very closely. "It is very interesting," he said, "but you do not seem to be the same person who offered me a ride several hours ago."

Jason smiled. "'Offered' is a pretty generous word, wouldn't you say? I wasn't in the greatest of moods a few hours ago, to be honest. Sorry if I came off like an asshole. I just kind of wanted to be alone."

"It is not a problem," Hector said. "Most people who are running away want to be alone."

"Running away? What are you talking about?" Jason was surprised to hear Hector describe him in that way, especially since he was right. "You think I'm running from the cops or something?"

Hector smiled. "In my experience, most people who are running are not running from the law. There are many things in life that are much more difficult to deal with. At least the laws usually are clearly drawn and defined. In our personal lives, the lines are much less clear." He looked down and ran his hand over the tabletop. "This is very nice—it's real wood, not a veneer. I like real wood. In a different life, I would have liked to be a carpenter. Working with wood truly is a gift." He picked up the menu and started to read.

Jason looked at him for several moments before he turned his attention to the menu. It seemed that Hector was much more observant than he had given him credit for. He hated it when people were so perceptive—it was another thing that always put him on the defensive. He wasn't comfortable with people knowing too much about him unless he chose for them to know. He was impressed by the depth that he saw in Hector's aspect. His face was thin with very prominent lines everywhere—in the cheeks, under the eyes, on the forehead, on the chin. It was easily one of the most expressive faces that Jason had ever seen, and it was framed by short jet-black hair that had no grey in it at all in spite of his age. Hector's eyes were deep black and shiny like obsidian, and Jason wondered what Hector would look like if he smiled.

"Hey, Hector," he asked, and Hector looked up. "Do you ever smile?"

Hector shook his head. "No, I do not. I have no sense of humor, so there is nothing to smile at."

Jason laughed, and he half-expected Hector to laugh along with him at the joke. Hector, though, just looked back at the menu with no perceptible change in the look on his face.

"Smart ass," Jason said with a smile, and Hector looked up and finally smiled. His eyes lit up when he did so, and all of the lines of his face moved to make his face cheerful and friendly and inviting.

"Yes, I am," Hector said. "Thank you."

"Have you decided yet?" Jenny asked, and Jason jumped at her voice—he hadn't seen her approach the table.

"I don't think *mi amigo* here has even looked at the menu yet," Hector said. "He prefers talking to eating."

Jason looked at Jenny and smiled. "I'm sorry," he said quickly. "Could you give me a couple more minutes?"

"Absolutely," she said with a smile. "I'm not going anywhere for a few hours."

Jason examined the menu and found a plate that sounded good. When he looked up, he saw that Hector was staring at him.

"What?" he asked.

"Nothing," Hector said. Jenny came back and they ordered. When she left, Hector took a drink of his coffee. "You seem to be a good person," he told Jason, "so I will give you some advice. It is very good advice, too. It is okay to run away from things if you are willing to leave them behind completely and forget about them. But if you carry them around with you for the rest of your life, then it is best that you not run away."

Jason smiled, but there was no humor in his face. He picked up his fork and looked at it closely for a few moments before replying. "It sounds like good advice," he said finally, "but there are some things that you can't leave behind. Some things are with you whether you want them to be or not."

Hector shrugged. "That may be so. Some things always come with us, like our hands or our feet. But there are many things that we choose to keep with us, like our anger or our thoughts about other people. Those we can leave behind. But it is just advice. You can keep it with you and use it as you will."

"Thanks."

"You are welcome."

They sat in silence for a couple of minutes, looking at the salt and pepper shakers, looking at the ketchup bottle, looking at the pictures and carvings of cows and pigs.

"You were telling me about when you were a kid," Jason said finally. "After your father died, and you were living with your mom and sister in Pocatello."

"Yes, I was. That was before I fell asleep." He looked down at his hands, and Jason expected him to continue. Hector didn't say anything more.

Jason sighed, exasperated. "You really are a smart ass, aren't you?" he demanded.

Hector smiled. "You are a fast learner."

"Well, are you going to tell me some more? It was a pretty interesting story."

"Do you think so? That is good, when one finds another's stories to be interesting. The most important interest that we can foster in life is an interest in our fellow human beings and their stories." Hector sighed. "If more of us were able to tell our stories to others who would truly listen, perhaps there would be much less crime and anger in the world."

Jason thought about that for a moment. "Yeah, you're probably right. We all want to share our stories, don't we? But usually no one wants to hear them because they're too busy living out their own stories."

"No," Hector said quietly but firmly. "Most are not busy living out their stories—they are busy avoiding their stories. Living in ruts and doing the same things over and over is not creating a story—it is much like a bad television series that tells the same story every week. Perhaps a name changes, or a store changes, or the place that they live changes. The writers of such stories simply copy stories that have come before. They do not use their imaginations, and they are not willing to take any risks. Most of us are afraid of creating stories, for true stories demand passion and risk and pain and putting our hearts on the line where someone might step on them. When Thoreau said that most people lead lives of quiet desperation, he was not talking only of the people in his own time—things have only gotten worse since he wrote those words."

"I never thought about it that way. I guess you're right. All of the stories that I really like have passion and risk and all that."

"If by 'all that' you mean trials and mistakes and redemption, then yes, you are right."

"That's pretty intense. By that standard, you'd have to say that most of us aren't even living at all."

"Or at least, most people aren't creating any sort of stories with the lives that they are leading. To create a story, one must give all one has to something, and few people are willing to dedicate themselves to something with all that they have."

"Because we're afraid of failure? Is that what keeps us from taking risks?"

Hector shrugged. "I cannot speak for all people. Usually, *amigo mío*, most people are more afraid of success than they are of failure. Just as I was many years ago. But I believe this is our food coming now. I will tell you the story as we eat."

"Here you go, gentlemen," Jenny said as she put the plates in front of them. "I'll be right back to warm up your coffees."

"Thank you very much, Jenny," Hector said. She smiled. "It is important to use people's names," Hector said to Jason when she left. He poured ketchup on his hash browns, bowed his head for about five seconds, then started to eat.

"When I was angry," he said after his first bite, "I was living no story at all. I was so focused on myself and what made me angry that I was not a person who was contributing anything to anyone. I went to school and my teachers were very nice to me, but I did not want them to be nice. They could see that I had much potential, but they also could see that I was coming nowhere near reaching it. They also knew about my family situation, and I think they felt sorry for me. One teacher used to bring me clothes, and that made me even more angry. I took them because I needed them, and because my mother needed me to take them, but they made me feel that I was not a normal person with a normal life. I made no friends during those years.

"I know now how much it hurt my mother to see me hurting so much, and she wanted more than anything in the world to help me. But she could not. I was not ready to be helped, so no matter what she did, it changed nothing. These eggs are very good."

Jason stopped in mid-bite, his fork at his mouth, caught off-guard by the sudden shift in topic. "Yeah, they are," he said. "This is one of the best omelets I've ever had."

"And the hash browns are very good too, no?"

Jason looked down at his plate. "Yeah. They're good."

"There are so many things that one can do with a potato. It is one of the most versatile foods in the world. French fries, hash browns, mashed potatoes, baked potatoes, potato bread, potato pancakes, potato chips. It is almost a miracle how many dishes one can prepare with the potato. One cannot do so many things with broccoli."

"I guess not."

Hector was quiet for a few minutes as he ate calmly, and Jason didn't know how to get him back to his story without seeming pushy or being rude. He wanted to hear more, but he didn't want to make Hector uncomfortable. On the other hand, he didn't want not to hear more.

"Aren't you going to go on with your story?" he finally asked. Hector looked at him with the most patient obsidian eyes in the world.

"Of course I am. But we have no hurry, do we? For stories, there is always time, I believe."

"Yeah, but now you've got me interested. What did your mother do? What kinds of things did you do when you were so angry all the time?"

Hector smiled slightly, looking Jason in the eyes as if he were looking at an old friend. "I did many things that were very stupid. But as I told you, I did not take my anger out on other people, but on myself. The person who suffered the most from my anger was me, yet I was so caught up in myself that I never thought that other people could be suffering on my account, simply because they loved me. When one loves another, it is very hard to watch that other person hurt himself.

"I would not participate in any activities at the high school because I believed that no one would want me to be part of them. I was a very good writer when I was young, and one of my teachers tried to convince me to write for the school newspaper. I would not do it. I thought that no one on the paper would want me to work with them, for they already had all the people they needed. If they were to let me work on the paper, they would just be doing me a favor. That is how I thought then. I was very stupid."

"You can't say that," Jason protested. "You were in pain. You had just gone through a great loss."

"I cannot say that?" Hector asked with a smile.

"You know what I mean!"

"But you do not know what I mean. I was very stupid. I did many stupid things. The fact that my father had died does not change the fact that I did many stupid things during those years. I hurt people and I hurt myself. Stupid is stupid. If you try to give it another name, then you are just not admitting that some people can be stupid, some for very long periods of time.

"Many people have suffered losses just as great as mine, and many more losses that were much, much worse, but not all of those people acted as I acted. I still had my mother and my sister who loved me, but I turned my life into an awful experience only because I was feeling sorry for myself. My toast is soggy. Is yours?"

Jason looked down at his plate. "I guess," he said.

"My mother was very worried about me, and she often would talk to me about the way I was acting. 'Hector,' she would say, 'I understand what you are going through, but I also know that you must go on with your life and not let what happened rob you of your youth. If you continue to hurt yourself this way, you will become a very bitter and a very unhappy man. It would be the worst thing that could happen to me to see you stay so unhappy for the rest of your life.' She spoke only from love, and do you know how I reacted? I was so stupid that I told myself that she couldn't understand how I felt, that she had no idea what it was like to be me. My mother had just lost her husband, a man she loved very deeply, yet I thought she could not understand the depths of my pain. And I was even more stupid because I believed myself when I told myself such stupid things."

"You're still pretty hard on yourself," Jason said. "You're judging yourself pretty harshly right now."

"No, *mi amigo*," Hector said, a surprised expression on his face, "I am not doing such a thing at all. I am merely observing the Hector that I used to be when I was so stupid. It is not judgment. I am quite happy with who I am now. I have reached a point at which I do silly things, and sometimes stupid things, but at least now I usually do not hurt other people with my stupidity."

"So you're not the same person you were back then?"

Hector looked amazed. "How can I be? I have almost seventy years now, and he had less than twenty. We are completely different people, are we not?"

Jason thought for a few moments. "I suppose so. It seems to make sense, but. . . ."

"But it is not how you have always thought about such things. Do not worry—you will get used to it. It is very difficult sometimes to think that we might have been thinking of things in wrong ways for so many years of our lives. Many people still thought the world was flat after it was explained to them that it was not. My sister, too, was upset with me during those years, mostly because of the way that I was making my mother feel.

"My sister and I never got along very well. I do not know why—it seems to me that given the way that we lived and because we had only each other so often, we should have been much closer than we were. But there was something very different in our relationship that I never understood until much later. I believe it was because I was the older child, and she thought she should have been. She was born to be a mother, my sister was, yet she did not understand that I was not born to be her child.

"My mother and father thought that it was funny, sometimes, that my sister would mother me so, and that probably made me resent it even more. She used to tell me when to do my chores, when it was time to do my homework, when I was doing something wrong. She was two years younger than I was, yet she would smile and tell me how well I was doing when I brought my report cards home from school. I didn't want to hear anything from her about how I was doing, good or bad. So when she would do that I would get angry with her, which would get my mother angry with me. And that would get me even more angry with my sister."

"What was your mother like? You keep talking about her, but you don't say much about what kind of person she was."

"I have told you—she was a saint. Was your mother not a saint?"

"Of course she was, until I got old enough to understand a lot of what was going on. But what did she do? How did she act? What was she like?"

Hector didn't reply for several very long moments. Jason felt him searching, looking for something that could explain one person to another person.

"When I was fourteen," Hector finally started, "two years before my father died, Ana Maria came home from school and she was crying very hard. She said that a little boy had hit her and spit on her and called her names like 'spic' and 'wetback,' names that I had been called a few times but which did not bother me all that much. They bothered my sister, though, and my mother took her in her arms and comforted her. As she held her there, I couldn't imagine a more peaceful sight, for my mother was the very picture of peace and calm and love. The sunlight was coming in through the window from behind her, and I remember sitting on the couch and watching them, feeling that deep sense of peace myself, loving my mother more than ever. In a few minutes my sister had cried herself to sleep in her arms, and my mother brought her very gently to the couch and lay her down on it, whispering to her the whole time. She kneeled down next to my sleeping sister and kissed her on the forehead, and I could see in her eyes all of the peace that she had just caused Ana to feel.

"Then she stood up and turned to me and I almost yelled out in fear, because her eyes were now filled with an anger such as I had never seen before. 'I need you to watch Ana Maria,' she told me, and her voice which had just been filled with peace and calm and loving words was now filled with a rage that matched that in her eyes. 'I am going to that school and I am going to find out who could do such a thing to my daughter, and why nobody did anything about it.'

"I was speechless. I watched in awe as she went calmly to the closet and got a sweater, then came over to me and kissed me on the forehead. I was even a bit afraid because she seemed like a bomb about to explode, but when she touched me I felt none of her anger at all, only love. I knew that if my father had been that angry, he would be yelling very loudly and even throwing things around the room, but my mother was completely in control of herself. I think it was the control that gave me the most fear. I could see just how much anger she had, but if I had not known her as my mother I would not have seen it at all. I was afraid for the people at the school as she went out the front door. I watched her through the window as she walked away, and I could see the energy and tension that she walked with. I felt that I should call my father and tell him, or call the school and warn them all to leave before she got there, but I was only fourteen, so of course I did nothing.

"She came back almost two hours later, and I could see that she was satisfied with what she had accomplished. She never spoke another word of the incident to me, or even to my sister, but I knew on that day that if I ever needed anyone to support me in any way, my mother would be there for me with all of her heart and soul. I could not imagine anyone standing up against that kind of anger without being very, very afraid of what might happen. And she seemed to have no fear of anything, especially when her children were involved.

"In a store once, I dropped a jar of pickles that I was carrying for her. A man from the store was standing very near to me, and he turned around and saw what had happened. He said, 'That was a very stupid thing to do.'

"'Don't you ever talk to my son that way!' my mother said immediately. 'Everyone has dropped something in their lives, and I will not allow you to insult my son for a simple mistake.' I thought we were in trouble for sure, but the man backed down. 'I'm sorry, ma'am,' he said. 'I meant nothing by it.'

"'If there is no meaning behind the words,' my mother answered, 'then perhaps they should not be said at all." I have always remembered those words. They were full of wisdom—I recognized that, even then. My mother was a simple woman with very little schooling, but she was a very wise woman."

"She sounds it," Jason said. "She sounds like a very marvelous woman."

"Of course she was marvelous. She was a saint. I told you that." Hector sounded surprised that Jason could have forgotten such a thing.

"Right—you're right. Sorry about that. I forgot."

"Here you go, gentlemen," Jenny said as she came back with the check and refilled their coffees. "I hope that you have a very nice trip, wherever you're heading."

"I am going to Pocatello," Hector told her. "And Jason is going to Seattle. Thank you for your kind wishes."

"You're very welcome," Jenny said with a smile. "Drop by if you're ever in the area again."

"Will do," Jason said, pulling some cash out of his pocket. Hector looked at the check and then gave nine dollars to Jason.

"This is what I owe," he said. "With a tip."

"You're a pretty big tipper," Jason said.

"Yes, I am," Hector replied.

"I am sometimes," Jason said. "I guess I have to be in the mood to leave a big tip."

"I am always in the mood to do something nice for other people. Besides, I am old, and I cannot take my money with me when I leave. I might as well pass it on to nice people."

"Yeah, you're right. It's easier to say than to do for me, though." Jason added his money to Hector's and pushed it all under his plate. "Let's get out of here and on the road. It's about that time."

"Let me use the bathroom first, and I will be right out. I do not want to make you stop any more than you have to."

"Sounds good. I'll meet you outside."

As he stood, Jason's legs once more reminded him of the abuse he was putting them through, and he stretched a bit as soon as he got outside. The sun was now up much higher in the sky, and the night was long since gone. He felt the sun's warmth on his cheek and he breathed deeply of the morning air, wishing it were a bit fresher but willing to take what he could get. He looked over towards the highway where the cars and trucks were speeding by, and he felt the road calling him, pulling him. He always felt that way when he was traveling, as if the road had some sort of power over him. He never liked stopping, even though he knew he had to. He always had to force himself to stop for food and for gas and for coffee—if it were up to him, he never would stop on any trip he took, as long as he was doing the driving. It was different when he was in the passenger's seat; then, he felt like stopping all the time. Hector came out of the restaurant.

"It's a beautiful morning," Jason said, looking up at the clear sky above them.

"Yes, it is," Hector agreed. "It is a beautiful morning to be on the road, especially with the sun behind us."

"You've got that right. It would be a real bitch if we were driving into it." Jason looked at his watch. It wasn't even seven yet, even though after the long night of driving he felt like it should be noon. If he had still been at home, he wouldn't even have been awake yet. "You know," he said, "it's a shame that so many people miss the mornings. They never get up in time to see it and feel it. Mornings are pretty beautiful. Hell, I never see the mornings unless I'm on some sort of trip or something."

Hector looked at him closely. "You are right—mornings are beautiful. They are the symbols of new birth and new beginnings. Every day we have the opportunity to start everything new, yet we almost never take the chance."

"You really believe that? That every morning's a new start? Seems to me that we bring too much of yesterday's crap into today for us to be able to start all over again."

"When you say 'we,' do you mean you?"

Jason laughed. "Probably."

"We bring to each day what we wish to bring to the day. That is all."

"Yeah, but what if you have a whole bunch of work left over from the day before? You're not really starting all over again—you're just finishing up whatever you didn't finish the day before, aren't you?"

Hector smiled. "Are you?"

"Of course you are."

"Is it not possible that the first part of the work was yesterday's work, and the rest is today's? Work is not like a football game that must be finished on the same day it is started. Just because we start a task today does not mean that all of that task is today's work. Sometimes we must be patient and let the work tell us how long it needs to be done well."

"That makes sense, I guess." Jason got into the car, and Hector got in on the other side. "I still think we bring too much of our yesterdays into today."

"I believe many people do, but not everyone. Besides, is it not possible that that is not a bad thing?"

Jason backed the car up. "I guess not." He started forward and pulled into the gas station right next to the restaurant. "I might as well fill up right here," he told Hector. "I'll be quick." He jumped from the car and pulled his wallet from his back pocket, taking out his credit card and swiping it through the slot in the pump. He was getting anxious now that he had been back in the driver's seat, anxious to get back on the road and moving once more. They had been in the restaurant much longer than he had thought they would be, and he wanted to start putting more miles between him and New Hampshire.

He shook his head at his own thoughts as he pumped the gas. Hell, he was in no hurry. No one was waiting for him, no one knew where he was going. He didn't have to be anywhere at any particular time. It was actually the first time that the fact sunk into his mind—he was completely free to go anywhere he wanted and to do anything he wanted to do. He wanted to cut all ties behind him, and he wasn't exactly looking forward to creating new ties ahead of him, so he had no schedule at all, nothing to keep him tied to any course of action or even direction of movement.

Chapter Four

The tank filled quickly, and very soon he was back behind
the wheel and out on the Interstate. Jason felt comfortable
moving at seventy miles an hour along with the other cars,
all going in the same direction on the same highway to
different destinations. He felt comfortable being in motion,
and he felt satisfied to be moving away from yesterday.

"Tell me some more about your mother," he said to
Hector. "She sounds like a really nice mom to have had."

"You have told me nothing about your mother," Hector
said quietly.

Jason glanced over at Hector, who was looking out the
window to his right at the landscape that they were flying
by. "There isn't much to tell, to be honest," he said. "I've
never really known her well. She wasn't around much. In
the early eighties most people were doing their best to climb
any corporate ladder they could get a foot on, and both my
mom and dad were pretty much absentee parents. I was
what was called a latchkey kid, until they started making
enough money to hire a nanny. My mother was a buyer for
a big department store, so she spent a lot of time traveling
to trade shows and stuff. I don't think she ever got home
before seven or eight o'clock on most nights. And she'd be
gone for four or five days at a time at least twice a month."

"That is sad. Was she happy?"

Jason thought for a moment. "I don't know," he finally
said. "Sometimes she seemed happy because she was
pretty proud of the job she had and her accomplishments
and all, but most of the time she seemed pretty worn out.
Both she and my dad were pretty awkward with my brother
and me. It was like they were always getting to know us,
like they had just met us all the time. They had to ask us
what sports we liked and what teams we liked and what kind
of music we listened to. Christmases were pretty pathetic,
though now that I look back on it, I guess they were pretty
funny. They didn't have much of a clue what we wanted.
When my little brother was four he loved the Ninja Turtles,
so one Christmas my dad actually bought him two live
turtles. Real live turtles, not the dolls or anything. Jake
named them Donatello and Raphael, even though he didn't
know what to do with them. My dad was impressed that a
kid his age was familiar with such famous artists."

"What was your mother like when you were young?"

"She was nice. She always seemed to be competing, though, and sometimes I used to think that she and dad were competing against each other. Who made the most money, who got the best promotions. Which one us kids liked better. I mean, they were both really successful in their careers, and I admire them for that, but they honestly weren't much as parents. If it wasn't for our nanny, I don't know what I would have done. I probably would have grown up without any affection at all."

"What was her name?"

"Patricia. Patricia Richardson. She was older than my mother, and she didn't let us get away with any crap, but she was the one who was there for us when we needed someone to calm us down or bring us up. I broke my leg falling out of a tree once when I was like eight, and my mom and dad were both out of town. So Patricia took me to the hospital and got me all fixed up. She took me home and set me up in bed with all sorts of pillows and blankets and stuffed animals—it was like I had become king of the house or something. It was pretty awesome, and my little brother was actually wishing that he had broken his leg—he said it wasn't fair that I got all the attention. I told him it was to make up for all the attention that he had taken away from me when he was born and he was the new baby. I don't know what happened to her, though. We moved away from Boston when I was eleven, and we never saw her again. That was sad. I remember wishing that we could have left my mother or father behind and taken Patricia with us. I even asked my parents if I could stay in Boston and live with Patricia. I don't think they liked that too much."

"Did you see your parents more after you moved?"

"Sort of. We moved to New Hampshire, to Concord, which was much smaller than Boston. To us, it was tiny, but I guess it was a decent-size town. My parents said we moved because they wanted to live in a place where we actually could be a family. I'm not quite sure what happened, though—within two years my father moved out and they were getting a divorce. I think my dad might have been seeing someone, because he remarried pretty quick after the divorce."

"Perhaps they just didn't know what it meant to live together as husband and wife."

"That's very possible. They were always on each other's nerves. My brother and I used to wish that they would take their old jobs, go away and hire Patricia again. My mom ended up taking a job that paid much better for the money, but she had to hire an almost-live-in maid to take care of the house and be there when we got home from school, because she was back to traveling a lot. That's just the way she was. But that maid didn't live with us, so it wasn't the same as with Patricia."

"That sounds very sad. Then you didn't really know your parents."

"Nope. Still don't. I never knew much about them—just that they were mom and dad. But I never knew anything about when they were kids or anything like that. In a way I always figured that they never had been kids, 'cause they didn't even know what it was like to have fun and just hang out and do stuff. They were very driven. They thought that was good."

"And your parents never knew you."

Jason thought about that for a few moments.

"I guess not. That's pretty sad. For me and for them. And for my brother, too. Maybe that's one of the things that I'm carrying around with me—resentment that my parents never made an effort to get to know me, their son. Or my brother. Boy, I hope that didn't screw me up for life. Then I wouldn't have anything to look forward to, would I?"

Hector laughed. "When we are screwed up, we choose to be screwed up. We can choose to unscrew-up ourselves."

"'Unscrew-up ourselves'? What the hell kind of word is that?"

"A word that sounds very appropriate. It is more accurate than any other words that I know. Life can get very boring if we limit ourselves just to what other people say we should know and use. Like words. But you have no good memories of your mother? Or your father?"

"Well, yeah. There were times when we all seemed pretty happy. Like one vacation that we took somewhere at a beach. I think it was on an island, but I don't remember exactly. We flew down there as a family, all four of us, and we stayed in this really cool hotel with a huge pool with slides and diving boards right in the middle of it. I thought it was pretty weird to have a swimming pool when we were only a couple of blocks from the beach, but I definitely spent more time in the pool than I spent in the ocean. The salt water made me skin feel all weird when it dried, and it tasted horrible.

"We went for a lot of long walks that vacation. I think we were there two weeks. We played miniature golf, we rode on the bumper cars, we did all sorts of stuff. Mostly for me and Jake, the great part was just being together as a family. I think that was the only time in our lives that we actually spent a whole lot of time with our parents and enjoyed it. I know that I came to the end of those two weeks wishing they would never end. I knew as soon as we went home that things would be back to the way they always were, even if I hoped inside that they'd change because of the vacation. I'm not sure what Jake thought about it—he and I never talked all that much. You'd think that we would have been the best of buddies since we pretty much only had each other, but we weren't. Kind of like you and your sister, I guess."

"Yes, it is very much like us. It is funny how sometimes the people we should be the closest to are the people we keep farthest away, no?"

"Yeah, it is. I mean, I liked my brother well enough, and we never fought with each other that much, but we also never really wanted to hang out with each other. We actually both preferred being alone, usually, to hanging around together. I've always felt kind of bad about that. I always felt I should have helped him out more, should have supported him and encouraged him more. After all, I was the oldest. I probably could have helped him out quite a bit."

"I am curious," Hector said. "If you have pleasant memories of your parents, then why is it that you hold on to the less-pleasant memories?"

"Hell, I've got to be realistic. It would be crazy to pretend that my family was this happy loving family when I was a kid."

"But I did not say to pretend. When do you feel better—when you are thinking of the happy memories or the memories that make you sad and angry?"

"Is that a trick question? The happy ones, of course."

"Then why do you choose to focus on the other ones when you know that they make you feel bad? And that you could make yourself feel better by focusing on the other ones? Perhaps you do not want to allow yourself to feel better?"

"Now why wouldn't I want to feel better?"

"Because then you have no one to blame for where you have been in your life."

Jason shook his head, afraid that Hector might have a valid point. "It's not that easy," he said. "You make it sound super-simple, but it's not."

"It is not?" Hector asked, bemused. "Have you tried?"

"It would be pointless to try to focus on just the positive memories. It would be impossible."

"Have you tried?"

"Hell, Hector, you're impossible. And persistent. No, I haven't tried. I don't enjoy taking on hopeless tasks."

"You do not get my point, *mijo*. How do you know that it is a hopeless task if you never try to accomplish it. Many people said that landing a man on the moon was a hopeless task."

"Okay, okay—I'm just assuming that it would be a hopeless task. Maybe someday I'll try it, and when I do I'm going to look you up and say, 'See, I told you—it was a hopeless task, but you talked me into doing it anyway.'"

Hector laughed. "Of course you will. You already have made up your mind, have you not? If you already have decided that you will fail, then you shall fail. And you shall come to me and say, 'Hector, I have failed, just as I predicted I would, and because I predicted I would.'"

Jason thought for several long moments, knowing that there had to be a good comeback to what Hector had just said, but unable to come up with one. He was afraid that Hector might be right, but he didn't want to admit that possibility aloud.

"Tell me more about your mother," he said finally. "Now that you've heard about mine, you can tell me more about yours. Your stories are much more interesting than mine are. I haven't even made any stories yet—I've had nothing but a boring, safe life."

"But you have not even told me your mother's name, Jason," Hector said quietly.

"I haven't?" Jason asked, amazed that he could have neglected such a detail. "Her name's Nora. My dad's name is Richard."

"Thank you. You are wrong, by the way, about the stories. You have stories, and they are interesting. You just have not learned yet how to tell them. When I tell you stories about my mother, I am telling you about someone I love very dearly. It is that love that makes the story interesting, even if the details are not very interesting in themselves. I can tell you a very boring story, but if I tell it with love, you will want to hear it."

"I don't know about that—maybe if I wanted to go to sleep or something. I'm not one for putting up with boring stories, Hector."

"Then I shall tell you more about my mother, for there is nothing about my mother that is boring, to me or to anyone else. She was a woman who lived her life with great passion, and a very passionate life may be tragic, and it may be difficult, but it is never empty.

"After my father died, she had many problems with me because of my anger. My anger made me very quiet and very withdrawn, and no one was able to convince me that I should be easier on myself. I think that many people felt that I was never able to get over my father's death, but that was not it. I used to lie awake at night and think about the people who pushed my mother and sister and me away after all that my father had done for them. All my life my parents had taught us about loyalty, and I believed that there was honor in loyalty, and that people who helped each other were loyal to each other. It was a very idealistic way of seeing things. I used to lie in bed and think of myself going to their offices or to where they worked or lived and telling them exactly what they were—heartless, evil men who made their money and their livings by hurting other people. I would yell at them in my mind, calling them filthy traitors, and there in my mind I would see them realize the truth behind my words. They would fall to their knees and beg forgiveness, telling me that they would make it up to my mother and sister, and I knew that my mother and sister would be grateful to me and admire me for the strength and courage that I showed in confronting those evil people.

"When I would come back to my senses, I sometimes would find that I was gripping the sheets or the blankets very tightly in my hands. I would feel silly, and I would let go of them and then be even more angry with myself for the cowardice I showed by not doing the very thing I fantasized about doing. I would never face such people, I would tell myself, for I was not brave enough to do so. And for that I felt that I deserved my own anger.

"One time my mother asked me why I took part in no extra activities at the school. I tried to tell her that I was not interested, that there was nothing at school that I wanted to do. She knew that I wanted to write, and she asked me why I did not become a part of the school newspaper. 'Hector,' she said to me, 'that would give you the opportunity to share your gifts with others, to give something to the world instead of only taking. We're not in this world just to take,' she said, 'but to give back to the world of the special gifts that we've each been given.'

"'Nobody wants my gifts,' I told her very fiercely, and I can still remember the shame that I felt for talking to my mother that way. 'Nobody wants me around,' I said, 'so why would they want me to share my gifts with them?' I was tempted to storm out of the room in order to make my point more dramatic, as most teenage boys like to do, but I knew that I could not be so disrespectful of my mother. I expected her to argue with me, and to tell me that I was wrong, and I was all ready to tell her that I was right and she was wrong, and that she did not have to live life in my skin, so how could she know what I felt and what other people felt about me?

"But she did not argue. That was very frustrating for me. I wanted to argue, for an argument would have given me more of a feeling of self-righteousness. It would have made it easier for me to continue to be angry. Instead, though, she did not say a word and she came to me and she held me. I could not believe what she was doing, for I knew that was exactly what I needed. But I also knew that I did not want what I needed, for I wanted to continue to be angry. So I fixed my gaze on a pillow on the couch and I refused to return her embrace. The pillow was one that she had made for my sister, and it had very ugly red flowers on it—I still can see the image in my mind. I stared and she held me, and I saw everything there was to see of the pattern on the pillow—the way that the flowers and the green leaves and the stems repeated themselves, how the image was designed to continue all along the fabric. I do not know how long she held me, but finally she let go, and she took me by the shoulders and she looked me in the eyes. I tried not to look back, but with my mother it was impossible not to return her gaze.

"'Hector,' she said in a very soft voice, 'please do not allow yourself to become so hard that you are no longer able to love, or to receive love. I want you to live your life and be happy doing so, and it will hurt me very much to see you unhappy when you have so many gifts for which you can be thankful.'

"I believe that was the start of my next death. It was as if there was a part of me that was very sick, and my mother had just injected the first medicine into my blood. It would take a long time for this death to happen, and it was a slow and painful death—but it finally did come.

"Before it came, though, my mother had an announcement for us—she was going to be married again, to a man with whom she worked in the factory. It confused me, because I thought that such an idea should make me even more angry, but it did not do so. I had almost no feelings at all when she told us about it. It was as if now that my anger was dying, I had no feelings at all. The wedding was a very good thing for all of us, for it meant that we would have the right to be in the country legally with no more problems with the Immigration department, no more need to register and deal with paperwork all the time. It was mostly important for my mother, though, who would not have to be alone any more, and who would not have to deal with her stupid son all alone any more. I wanted to be very, very angry, but I could not be. I knew James, and I knew that he was a very good man. I knew that he would be a very good husband for my mother, but I did not care whether he would be a good father for me or not. I already was almost old enough to leave the house, and I wanted to do that as soon as I could.

"The wedding took place in June. They were married in a small park in the town next to a small pond. My mother was absolutely beautiful in her new dress, and all of her friends from work were there. There was no family, for we had no family in Pocatello. James' family was there, and the friends from work also were his friends, of course.

"James had asked me if I would be his best man, which I know now was a very big honor. Then, though, I thought he was just trying to make me feel better about him marrying my mother. I told him no. It was another thing I wanted to be angry about, but there was no anger there. My mother took me aside some weeks before the wedding and asked me why I would not be the best man. I told her some stupid excuse—I do not even remember what I said—but she would not let me get away with it. 'Tell me truthfully, Hector,' she told me. 'I always have been honest with you, and I expect you always to be honest with me.' And she was right, she always had been honest with me. And I knew that because she was honest with me, I had to be honest with her. The problem was, I did not know for sure why I did not want to be the best man. I told her that.

"She did not know what to say. 'I suppose it's better to hear you say that,' she said to me, 'than many of the other things that you might have said to me. If I may ask you a favor, though, I would like to ask you to do this thing for me. I know that I have no right to ask any favors of you, but if you would grant me this, you would make me a very happy person.'

"I was astonished. How could my mother possibly have said that she had no right to ask any favors of me? It made no sense to me at all. I found her humility to be almost unbelievable, but I knew that anything my mother said, I had to believe, for it had to be true. It was very hard for me, but I told her that I would do her that favor. She almost cried from gladness, and for the first time in my life I saw very clearly just how much effect the things that I did had on other people. I always had thought that no one cared what I did or did not do, but in that moment a door opened and I was able to see life—my life—in a different way. And learning that lesson made me understand the pain that I had been causing my mother and sister for so long. Even though I had thought that I was affecting only myself with my anger, I really was hurting the people I loved."

He fell silent and looked out the window on his side of the car for a while. Jason also was quiet, not knowing what to say. He saw himself in much of what Hector had just said, but he didn't know what that meant to him. In a few minutes, Hector finally spoke.

"The trees here are very green," he said.

"Yeah, they are," Jason agreed. He paused several moments, but Hector didn't continue. Finally, he asked, "So how was it? How was it being the best man?"

Hector laughed. "Other than the very ugly suit that I had to wear? I think that someone must have stolen it from a dead man and then given it to me, for I do not believe that anyone who was alive ever would buy such a suit. It was brown plaid, all of it, the pants and the shirt and the jacket, and not a very nice plaid. It was the color of dirt. The people who made it must have been very drunk when they did so. Even my mother felt very sorry for me when she saw me in it. My sister just laughed. A lot. I don't think she stopped laughing, even when my mother was taking her vows. But none of us had seen it until the morning of the wedding, for the man who loaned it to me had taken it to the cleaners and had just picked it up that morning. He had told us that he had a perfect suit, just my size. I did not know if I wanted to kill him or myself while I was wearing it, but I do believe now that the clothes we wear can cause us to commit crimes. I almost did that day.

"But the most remarkable thing was that on that day, even with this suit from the devil, I was to meet the most amazing woman in the world and fall in love with her immediately. Unfortunately, she did not fall in love with me—I believe that it was because of the suit—but neither did she find me appalling, and at least I was able to see her a few times. And after those few times, then she started to fall in love with me as the memories of me wearing the suit faded in her mind. She was the beginning of the greatest story of my life, a story that still continues, even though she has long since passed on to whatever comes next for us."

"What was her name?" Jason asked.

"That's strange," Hector said, thinking deeply. "I cannot remember."

"You've got to be kidding me," Jason said. "You don't remember her name?" He couldn't believe his ears.

"I'm not sure. I believe it began with an 'M' or an 'N.' Or perhaps a 'P.'"

Jason looked over at him and caught Hector looking back at him out of the corner of his eye, the beginning of a smile on his lips. "Oh, man," he said. "You're putting me on, aren't you?"

"Yes, I am putting you on," Hector said with a laugh.

"You really had me going, too," Jason said. "You do that very well."

"Thank you very much," Hector replied. "I believe that if I were to come back to this planet and live another lifetime as a human being, I would choose to come as an actor. Not a movie star, but an actor upon the stage. There is something exhilarating about being someone else for a short time—not pretending to be someone else, but actually being someone else for as long as the play goes on. Actors tell us stories. When we know people, when we make friends, very few of us tell each other our stories. But when we see a play, we see stories being told. I love stories. My greatest story began when I met Leigh."

"So that was her name? This woman you met at the wedding?"

"Oh, no—I did not meet her at the wedding. I met her that day, but not at the wedding. I met her after the wedding. She was one of the women who were working as servers for the reception. The reception was held at a hotel, and she was working at the hotel part time to help her to pay for college. She was a student, studying to be a teacher, and from the moment I saw her at the reception, I could not take my eyes off of her. I was fortunate that the angry part of me had begun to die, for I know that if I still had been angry, she would have had no desire to get to know me at all."

"What did she look like?"

"She was not a woman whose pictures would be on the covers of magazines, but she was no less beautiful for that. Her hair was dark blond, and she carried herself with the grace of a swan. Her eyes were bright like the stars in the night, and her smile was perhaps the most wonderful thing about her. Her smile told a million stories all by itself, stories of love and compassion and peace and hope. It was a smile that would make you feel comfortable and happy, especially if it were directed your way. When I saw her smile as she worked, serving the people at the reception, I knew that I had to meet her. I approached her. 'What is your name?' I asked her. She looked a bit confused, then she looked down at her name tag. I had not even noticed that she was wearing one.

"'I'm Leigh,' she said, and I was glad that she told me, for I never would have pronounced her name correctly. How can L-e-i-g-h be pronounced the same as L-e-e? It still makes no sense to me, but then I had been speaking English even less time, so it was very confusing to me.

"'My name is Hector,' I told her, 'and your smile is the greatest treasure that I ever have had the honor of seeing.'"

"You told her that?" Jason asked. "Oh, my."

"I told her that. I was young, and I had no shame at the time. But even more importantly, I meant it. I truly did. I believe that I already had fallen in love with her by then, though of course I could not tell her that."

"What did she say?"

"She said, 'Thank you, Hector. That's very kind of you.' Just like that, as if she were a cashier in a supermarket and I were a customer she had never seen before. Very polite, but also very distant—perhaps 'cautious' is a better word."

"I probably would have been cautious, too, after a line like that."

"There was nothing wrong with the line. Besides, it was not a line, it was the truth."

"Sometimes truth can sound like a line."

"That is true. Then she said that she had to get back to work, for there was much work to do. I spent the rest of the evening trying not to look at her, for I did not want her to feel afraid of me, to feel that I would make problems for her. It was not easy to make her feel comfortable, though, when I was wearing such a bad suit. I wanted nothing more that to look at her and perhaps see her smile again, but I forced myself not to look. You see, back then I also felt my nationality very strongly, and I knew that many people in this country were suspicious of people from any other country, and I didn't know if she would see me as a human being or as a Mexican."

"I know what you mean—it can be terrible when people don't see you as a person, but as a member of a group that they don't like."

"It has happened to you, too?" Hector asked.

"Yeah," Jason answered quietly. "But go on with your story. You had to meet her if she became the love of your life. How'd you manage that?"

Hector regarded Jason for a moment before he replied. "It was very simple, really. I borrowed a yellow rose from my mother, and when the dancing began and they started cleaning up everything from dinner, I took the yellow rose to

Leigh and I told her, 'This is for you, out of gratitude for the smile that you have shared with us.'"

Jason moaned. "Oh, Hector. You really laid it on thick, didn't you?"

Hector looked over at him with a smile on his face. "You should try it sometime, *amigo*. There is nothing wrong with making another human being feel good by sharing compliments."

"But she had to see right through you, didn't she?"

"What was there to see through? I was being sincere, and she could see that. Perhaps the words were melodramatic, perhaps I was not the most gifted at finding words to express the way I felt inside. But I spoke with sincerity, and she could see that. It was not the words that caused her to agree to have lunch with me that weekend, but the sincerity with which I spoke them, and the honesty that she could see in my eyes."

"Are you sure it wasn't pity for you because of the suit?"

Hector laughed. "That could be, my friend. But I believe it was because I was being true. So many people are afraid to say what they truly feel because they fear that others will not believe them or will make fun of them, but what is life if we cannot speak what is truly on our minds? How often do you not say something because you are afraid of how another person will react?"

Jason thought for a moment. "Quite a lot, I guess. I'm always wondering what other people will think if I say something. I think most people are."

"And if most people are, then how many honest words are not being spoken in this world? What would this world be like if all people spoke honestly?"

"I don't know if I want to go there. Not all of the words that I hold back are exactly complimentary."

"Yes, there is that," Hector sighed. "Of course, we cannot always go around speaking our minds honestly. What a shame that is." He sighed again, then looked out the window.

"You don't mind if we stop at this rest area ahead, do you?" Jason asked. "I have to go to the bathroom."

"No, that is fine with me. I am carrying around more of the coffee than I need, and it is asking to get out of me."

Jason laughed. "That's one way of putting it."

They rode the next five minutes in silence until Jason took the exit for the rest area. He felt the power of the engine as he downshifted to slow down, and he felt in perfect sync with the vehicle. Hours earlier, he had felt that the car was somehow his partner in isolation, helping him to hide from the world, but now he felt a much more positive connection. He knew that he had Hector to thank for that.

"This is a very nice car," Hector said, surprising Jason. "It rides very smooth, and it feels like it knows us and wants to take us where we are going. It lives up to its name—Cavalier. *Caballero*."

"I suppose it does at that," Jason said. "I'm pretty happy with it. It certainly gets me where I'm going with little fuss, and I don't think you can ask more out of a car than that."

"No, I don't think so."

"Thank God for rest areas," Jason said as he and Hector made their way towards the bathrooms. "If it wasn't for these places, I guess we'd have to stop at gas stations all the time just to relieve ourselves."

"Where there is need, human beings usually will do their best to fill that need. It is one of the many positive things about our species. We are always looking for ways to help people whom we never will know. The people who built this area never will meet you or me, yet they have built this here for the many thousands of people who will stop here to use it."

"Pretty amazing, isn't it? It's too bad all people can't be like that, though. There are just as many people who do their best to destroy things and break things down."

"There are many such people, but I do not believe that there are just as many. I believe they are very few. When you watch the news or read the newspapers, you do not read about the good people who build rest areas. If I build this rest area, no one ever knows my name. If I burn it down, my name is in all the newspapers and my picture is on television."

"I never thought about it that way. You're right, though. It's pretty warped, isn't it?"

"It is very sad. What does a young person have to aspire to? They see the people doing good receiving no recognition, and the criminals and entertainers and the politicians on the news all the time. We all crave attention, and many people cannot be satisfied with getting little attention in their lives. They try always to get more, no matter how."

"Boy, you're right there. My brother and me, all we wanted was some attention from our parents, but we never got it. You know, Hector, you're pretty amazing. We're at a rest area, for God's sake—a place that exists for people to use the friggin' toilet—and you turn it into a philosophy lesson."

Hector laughed. "And what is wrong with philosophy, my friend? Who is to say that philosophy should be limited to the classrooms in colleges, when we can think just as deeply while sitting on a toilet?"

"I guess the problem is that when you're sitting on the toilet, you can't share your philosophy with nearly as many people. Maybe the guy in the next stall, but what are the chances that he even wants to hear what's going on in your mind? He's probably got his mind on other things."

"Philosophy," Hector said gravely, "must not always be shared to have value. There is no need for us to put our philosophies into a store window for other people to see and to criticize or to praise. Philosophy is just as personal as emptying our bladders or our bowels. Somehow, though, we start to think that others must validate our philosophies if they are to have any value. That is not true."

"Hmm. . . . That makes sense."

They went inside the bathroom, a stuffy-smelling room with stainless steel fixtures everywhere. Along one wall were three stainless steel sinks on the left and three stainless steel urinals on the right, and facing them were five stalls, all with closed doors that had little windows showing green by the handles, indicating that they weren't occupied.

"Well, Hector," Jason said, motioning to the room, "it looks like we've got the run of the place. Plenty of room to piss and philosophize all you want."

"Thank you. I must sit down now." He went to one of the doors and opened it, looking in. "I have found that in a place such as this, it is much better to look before you enter. One never knows what might be waiting."

"There's a disgusting thought. See you in a few." Jason moved to one of the urinals as Hector closed the door behind him.

When he was outside again, Jason stretched his arms as high into the sky as he could. He felt the cool breeze on his stomach where his shirt came untucked. For the first time in quite a few hours, he was alone, and he liked the feeling. For the slightest of moments he wondered if he had it in him to leave Hector's bag on the sidewalk and take off and enjoy the rest of his trip in the peace and quiet he had been looking forward to. Hell, he'd never see Hector again, and it wasn't like he'd be breaking any sort of law.

The thought didn't stay with him long, though. He liked Hector, and he liked listening to his stories. It would be cruel and cold-blooded to leave the man there, and Jason wasn't a cruel person. And Hector certainly didn't deserve to be treated that way.

Besides, he hadn't exactly been enjoying himself when he had been alone before he took on a passenger. "You're in it for the long run," he muttered to himself.

He figured he had quite a few more stories to hear over the next day or two, and it certainly was more interesting to listen to Hector talk about his life than it was to listen to all of the same CD's over and over again.

He walked slowly towards his car, stretching his legs with each step. He hopped up and down a couple of times, then when he reached his car he jogged slowly to the end of the parking lot. It felt good to run, and he could almost feel his heart pumping faster, his blood flowing faster. His mind cleared a bit, and he didn't feel as tired. He knew that he would have to stop for a couple hours of sleep sometime soon, but for now he was still feeling pretty good.

The breeze was perfect—just slightly cool on an already-warm day. It was the kind of day made for cruising down the highway with the windows wide open, but somehow he didn't think that Hector would enjoy that too much. He stopped and watched the leaves on the trees that provided a backdrop to the rest area. They were restless, blowing in the breeze as if they wanted to go somewhere, but they were stuck where they were.

"Sorry about that, leaves," Jason said aloud. "I sure am glad I'm not you. It must be hell to be stuck here all the time, I would guess."

He turned and jogged back to his car. Hector was just coming out of the bathroom.

Jason watched him approach, a seventy-year-old man who had become his traveling companion. Hector walked with a limp, favoring his left leg, but he walked with grace and a distinct dignity. This was a man, Jason would have guessed, who had accomplished much in his life and who was admired by the people who would love him. The dignity was unmistakable and not something that one could fake.

"You have not left me here to find my own way back to Pocatello," Hector said. "This is a good thing for me."

"I thought about it," Jason said, "but then I'd never find out about your marriage to Leigh. Besides, how could I leave you way out here in the middle of nowhere? You'd die of boredom before you could ever get a ride."

"Jason, if ever I am bored anywhere that I am, then I hope that I will die. That boredom would be of my doing. There is always something to make every place interesting. And if there's very little to make the place interesting, then we must make ourselves interested. Besides, this would be a very good place to develop my philosophy of life. The seat on the toilet is very comfortable, and the smell in there is not too bad."

Jason chuckled. "Too much information, Hector. That's simply much more than I needed to know. Look, do you want to walk around a bit and stretch? Get your blood flowing?"

Hector looked around. "Thank you, but I shall pass. At my age, my body appreciates it when I give it much rest. I believe I will continue resting it in the comfortable seat of the *Caballero*."

"Whatever butters your toast, then," Jason said. "Shall we be going?"

"That will be fine," Hector said, opening the passenger door. "And as we drive, perhaps you can tell me a story of your life."

Chapter Five

Jason laughed as he got into the car, and he waited until Hector was sitting comfortably with his seatbelt on before he replied. "First of all, I don't have any stories. And even if I did try to put some of my miserably ordinary experiences into story form, I'm pretty sure you'd find them far too boring—they'd either put you to sleep or kill you, or maybe even cause you to take your own life." He backed up, then started towards the exit where the rest area once more emptied onto the highway. He enjoyed accelerating, shifting when the car needed him to shift, feeling the growing power of the engine as he pushed it harder.

Hector watched the road before them.

"You do have stories, Jason," he said. "We all have stories. The problem is that people your age never have been taught to tell them. How can they be taught, when their parents do not tell stories, either? The sad part is that one day you will have no stories to tell your children or your grandchildren, so they never will have the benefit of learning from your experiences. That is a shame."

"What makes you think that I'm ever going to have children, Hector? How do you know I'm not gay or something?"

Hector looked at him, a bit surprised at the challenging tone in Jason's voice. "Even gay couples often adopt children, do they not? Even if the children in your life are the children of your friends or your neighbors, they are still all of our children—it is up to all of us to nurture them and to share our experiences with them. Our stories help them to feel connectedness, help them to feel less lonely and isolated because they know that they share thoughts and feelings and experiences with other human beings. We must have our stories if we are going to pass on our experiences." He paused for a few moments. When Jason didn't reply, he turned to him again. "Are you gay?"

Jason looked back at him. "What do you think?"

Hector shrugged. "Yes, you are gay."

"How do you know for sure?" Jason asked.

"For sure, I know nothing. I have been surprised far too many times in my life ever to think that I know anything 'for sure.' But this thing I know, and I do not know how. It is not important how. When you are my age, there are things that you just know, if you keep your eyes and mind and heart open to knowing."

They rode in silence for several long minutes, in what was the closest they had come to an awkward silence since Hector had come on board. Jason kept his eyes on the road, on the mirrors, on the other vehicles that were sharing the road. Hector watched the scenery as it flew by; neither of them made any effort to continue the conversation until Hector began to speak.

"After I took Leigh to lunch that one day," he said finally, "she and I started seeing each other regularly. Soon my anger was completely dead, and it was replaced by a sort of worship of this woman who had come into my life and changed things so drastically. My mother, of course, had started the process of killing the anger, but it was my relationship with Leigh that allowed me finally to let it go completely. I cannot tell you how important it is to be able to let go of things like anger and jealousy and hatred and resentment—it is a lesson that it took me many years to learn, and I wish that I had not wasted so many years before I learned it.

"Leigh brought joy to my life. I was amazed that this beautiful woman could look at me with love in her eyes, that I could be the inspiration for one of her beautiful smiles. I never understood how it could be that just looking at me could make her smile, even though I knew from experience that just looking at Leigh could make *me* smile. Somehow, it was easy for me to see how she could make someone else smile, but it was impossible for me to understand why anyone—especially her—could be moved to a smile just by seeing me. It is a mystery that still puzzles me, though I have accepted that anything is possible in this world of ours.

"One afternoon after I had been seeing her for about a year, Leigh and I went on a picnic at a lake in the mountains. It was a long drive—she had the car, not I—but it was one of the most beautiful places that I ever had seen. It was a small lake at the foot of a majestic mountain that simply stood there, looking down at us and blessing us with its presence. We were surrounded by pine forest, and there was a soft breeze that was very cool, even in July, for we were high enough in the mountains that the temperature was much cooler.

"Leigh was wearing a lovely soft white dress that was not very practical, but was very exquisite. It made her look like a princess. It is hard for me to describe her, for I know her too well, and I knew her for more than thirty-five years. It is very hard for me to separate in my mind the Leigh that I last knew and the Leigh that I met when I was a young man. She was a little shorter than I, and her hair was a dark blonde. Her skin was fair, while mine was very dark, especially in the summer when I would spend much time in the sun. Her face was thin, and if I had to draw her nose and her mouth and chin, I would use sharp, clear lines to do so. Her lips were a bit pale, and they were always ready to turn up into a smile. Her eyes were a marvel to behold—they were very clear and sharp and I felt that they could look straight into my soul. They were very pale green, almost without color at all, I sometimes thought, and they were the most honest and loving eyes that I had ever seen, except for my mother's. And just like my mother, her eyes were normally smiling, but when she felt anger, her eyes were very, very frightening.

"She had made a picnic lunch, she had borrowed her parents' car, she had arranged the day—that was just the kind of person she was. She did not want to control other people, but she was willing to be the person to make plans and to follow through on them so that other people could benefit from her actions. I believe that is why she made such a special teacher.

"We spent many hours up there. We talked about everything, and she told me about her plans to be a teacher once she finished with college, and her plans to live in Pocatello all her life so that she could give back to the city that had given her so much. She wanted to teach the children and the grandchildren of her friends and her parents' friends and the friends that she would have in the future. She thought that by teaching children, she was giving the greatest gift to the world that she possibly could give. That was her special calling, she knew, and she wanted to use the gift to help people as much as she could.

"When she asked me what I wanted to do with my life, though, I had no answer for her. I had not thought of that at all before. My mother had tried to talk to me about it, but you know how it is when you talk things over with parents— you kind of think about the things, but there is not as much urgency in coming up with answers. When I was talking to Leigh, though, I felt that urgency. I wanted to give her an answer that would satisfy her, that would make her proud to know me and proud to be my friend. But I had no answer for her. That was probably the best thing that ever could have happened to me, for it was during that conversation that Leigh encouraged me to go to college so that I could learn about many different things and then decide what I wanted to do.

"My mother had mentioned college before, but I hadn't taken her too seriously. She had started to mention it during my angry years, and because I responded always in such negative ways, she gave up trying to convince me that I should do something that would be good for me. I cannot blame her for giving up. But by the time Leigh and I left the lake that afternoon, I was thinking already about starting college that fall. I had just finished high school and I had no plans. Leigh had just finished her first year of college. My mind was set on going home and applying to the college and looking for ways to pay for it, and suddenly I was looking forward to the future for the first time in a very long time.

"We stopped at a supermarket on the way home, for Leigh had to get something for her mother. I never will forget that time. We were very happy, smiling and enjoying each other very much. When we got into the store, though, we ran into Leigh's father. I never had met the man, but I guessed right away that he was Leigh's father because she said "Daddy" as soon as she saw him. I was very bright back then. But there was something wrong with her voice— it told me that she had been caught at something that she did not want to be caught at. He was looking at her with a very stern face, and I immediately did not like the man. I never had met him, but I never had wondered why. It truly did not matter to me. But when he looked at me, I knew right away why we never had met. He looked at me with contempt and with anger and with arrogance, and I knew he was looking at me that way because of the color of my skin, because of where my parents had been born. I was a Mexican, and among some people there was much prejudice against Mexicans back then. Now there is not so much—it is still all around us, but not so much as then.

"'I'll see you at home, Missy,' he said to her, and that was all of their conversation. He put down what he had been wanting to buy and he stormed out of the store. I looked at Leigh hopelessly, for I had no idea what I could do to make things better. I would have changed my skin color for her, but there was no way for me to do that.

"I still remember how bravely she smiled, and how sad the smile looked. 'It'll be okay, Hector,' she said quietly, and when she looked me in the eyes, I could see that she spoke the truth. And for the first time, even though we had been seeing each other for so long, I knew that she loved me. And I knew that I loved her. We bought what she needed to buy, and she even picked up the jar of pickles that her father had put down and she bought those, too. When she dropped me off at my house, she said, 'We'll be fine, Hector, don't you worry.' And then she kissed me, for the first time."

"Wait a minute," Jason protested, looking over at Hector with suspicion in his eyes. "You mean to tell me that you'd been seeing her for over a year, and you hadn't even kissed her yet? You've got to be kidding!"

Hector laughed loudly. "I know how that must sound to a young person of today, but you must remember that those were the end of the 1950's, and things did not happen so quickly then. Now, two people meet and they are often in bed the same evening, but back then, people took their time more. There seemed to be more time to take, too— everyone was not in such a hurry to do everything quickly all the time. Courtships lasted a very long time, and they were taken very seriously. I do not know which way is better— there probably is no better way at all—but the times were different, that is for sure.

"I saw her again a few days later, and she smiled broadly when she saw me. I knew that everything was okay. We were in the park, where we often met to go for walks. I asked her what had happened. 'Daddy told me that I couldn't see you any more, that no daughter of his was going to be seen with a Mexican. And he said "Mexican" like it was a dirty word. But Daddy can go to hell.'

"I laughed, but I was nervous. I didn't want her to be hurt. 'What did you tell him?' I asked her.

"She laughed softly, and then she spoke softly. 'I told him, "Daddy, you can go to hell." You should have seen the look on his face, to hear his loving daughter tell him something like that. Before he could answer me, though, I told him, "I don't know what you're trying to teach me by acting like a racist bigot, but that is most certainly a lesson I refuse to learn. I'm going to be teaching children about tolerance and humanity and brotherhood, and I am not going to teach them to be racists. So please don't try to teach me any lessons about bigotry and racism, because I don't want to learn those things. Especially from my own father." Then I went to my room before he could even answer.'"

Jason whistled softly. "Wow—what a perfect thing to say. That would shut me up real quick."

"Yes. And she went on to teach young people to be tolerant and to love their neighbors, not judge them. What would this world be like if every young person were to learn such lessons very early in their lives? What would this world be like if there were no people who judged others by the color of their skin or their language or their sexuality or the clothes that they wear?"

"That's hard for me to imagine," Jason said. "I haven't seen the model yet."

"I have not seen it, but I have imagined it. There are enough people who do not allow prejudice to warp their vision of the world for me to understand what it would be like if the world were full of this kind of person. While I taught at college, there were very few people on the faculty or the staff that showed any sort of prejudice, and it was a very nice world to be a part of. College teachers often are not the most skilled in social situations, but their minds tend to be very open. They tend to be very accepting of life and other people and other ways of seeing things. If only they would not tend to take any challenge to their credibility or their authority so personally, the college environment might be close to perfect."

"You taught college? What did you teach?"

"I taught Spanish, believe it or not. After Leigh talked me into going to college, I started that fall, and my advisor over the next two years convinced me to study Spanish. He said that there would be plenty of work for me as a teacher once I got my Master's degree. And he was correct—it was very easy for me to find work teaching about the language and literature in those days. I had the advantage of being a native speaker, of course, which helped me very much when I was looking for work, even though I have met many teachers who are not native speakers who are much better than I at teaching the language. Because it was a foreign language for them, they seemed to have studied the grammar more deeply than I. I think that I took the grammar for granted, as I had been speaking Spanish all my life. Also, I did not understand as well some of the difficulties that English-speaking people have when learning Spanish. The subjunctive is very difficult for most students."

"I never learned any languages," Jason said. "I took French in high school, but I was horrible at it. In college I got the bright idea to take Russian—I spent two semesters at it, and I got C's both semesters, but came out of it not even able to put together an intelligible sentence. It was pretty sad."

"Languages are not for everyone, my friend. I have had students who learn everything almost immediately, and I have other students who work very, very hard but learn almost nothing. Some students learn the grammar and vocabulary very well, but end up not being able actually to speak the language. It is a very interesting process to observe."

"There are a lot of things my mind isn't able to do, I'll tell you that much. My entire high school career consisted of me trying to catch up on work that I was behind on, and trying to pull my grades out of the 'F' range, which is where they tended to settle by the middle of every quarter. Half the time I was able to bring them back up, half the time I wasn't."

"That must have been very frustrating. Do you have some sort of Learning Disorder?"

Jason shook his head. "I don't know. I never got tested or anything like that. My parents used to just ground me, and I'd have to find ways around getting the bad grades. It really sucked. None of my friends ever seemed to have any problems with classes, and they weren't any smarter than I was. But I always had problems. No matter how much my teachers tried to help me, I couldn't ever get the grades. I mean, I understood the material and I didn't have any problems with the concepts, but when it came to taking tests or quizzes or writing papers or doing homework, I just bombed. All the time."

"I am surprised that you never were tested for these problems."

"Well, my parents thought that I was just lazy. My brother always did fine, so there shouldn't have been any problem for me, they thought. So I just hung in there the best I could and watched my brother and friends get A's and B's while I was constantly getting grounded for D's and F's. School wasn't my favorite thing in the world, obviously. I was surprised that I even got into college, but I think my father pulled in a favor or two from some friends of his. I actually passed most of my classes at college, mostly with C's, which surprised everyone, I guess."

"Grades are not the measure of the student. Unfortunately, most people seem to see them as the only measure of learning that has taken place. But they rarely show just how much a student has learned in a class."

"Yeah, you're right," Jason said. "I think the only thing that kept me from dropping out of school was the fact that I was learning a lot, and I really loved learning. I just couldn't prove to anyone that I was learning in the ways that they wanted to see the proof. Hey, it looks like we're driving right into a storm." He pointed through the windshield at a bank of ominous clouds that were filling the sky to the west ahead of them. They had appeared fairly quickly—he didn't remember a point at which he had first noticed them. They just seemed to be there all of a sudden.

"It looks like there is much rain in these clouds," Hector said, peering through the windshield. "This will be a very strong storm."

Jason smiled. "I love driving through storms. It's pretty awesome to drive through the heavy rain and have the windshield wipers going full speed just trying to keep up with the water, knowing that you're safe and sound and dry in this little compartment speeding down the highway. You don't even get wet, even when you're going through the worst storms. It's pretty cool."

"Yes, it is very impressive when we think of how protected we are from the elements. Some of us try to protect our emotions in much the same way."

"How? By driving through rainstorms?" Jason laughed.

Hector didn't answer immediately. He looked at Jason for a moment, then looked again at the approaching storm. "By putting their emotions into a little box inside of their minds in order to protect them from other people. If you can lock away your emotions, then you will not be hurt.

That is what people think. Sometimes I believe that most of us never get out of our cars—we always keep ourselves isolated from other people in order to protect ourselves from the rain and the snow and the thunder and lightning. But I think that we do ourselves much harm by isolating ourselves from others. The rain and snow can be beautiful to walk in and enjoy."

"I think you're right there, Hector," Jason agreed. "I know I do that. It's safer that way."

Hector looked at him quizzically. "What is safer?"

"You know, 'it.' Life, I guess. Living."

"But life never is safe. How can we make safe what is not meant to be safe?"

"You can keep yourself from getting hurt, that's for sure."

Hector chuckled. "And you can keep yourself from getting food poisoning by never eating. Only you will soon starve to death. There is an old saying that says that a ship in the harbor is safe, but that is not what ships are made for."

"I like that," Jason said. "I've got to remember that."

"There are many such sayings that we should remember. Most of the important ones, I have forgotten. I wish that I could remember them better, but I cannot."

"Yeah, I seem to forget most of the important stuff myself. Then I make the same mistakes over and over again, and I think, 'Oh, yeah—I should have remembered that!' Look at that grove of trees up there," he said, pointing to a spot ahead of them. "All of the trees that are farther away are in the rain, and you can hardly see them. It's moving in on us, that's for sure."

"Yes, it is," Hector agreed.

"I love this. It's like being at an amusement park on one of those rides that go into long dark tunnels. It's all about expectation and getting ready for something that promises to be really cool."

Just as he finished his sentence, the first drops of rain hit the windshield.

"Here we go," Jason said, sitting up straighter in his seat. He knew that he'd have to concentrate much harder once they were in the storm itself, and he put both hands on the wheel. "Do you like storms, Hector?"

"I like everything," Hector said simply. "I believe storms are among the most beautiful things in this world. They show the true beauty of power that is expended in a completely impersonal way. Storms do not do what they do to impress anyone, yet they are impressive."

"You can say that again. I think that if I had to do it over again, I'd like to be one of those people who study storms. You know, the ones who chase hurricanes and tornadoes and lightning storms to record everything that's going on. That would be such a cool job."

The rain was falling heavily now, and Jason had to raise his voice to be heard above the steady roar of the raindrops pelting against the roof of the car. He kept his eyes glued to the road ahead, which was now covered with a sheet of water. He could see no more than a hundred yards ahead, and his speed was down to forty. He focused on staying out of the grooves that held most of the water so that he had less of a chance of hydroplaning—the more he could stay on the actual pavement and off of the water, the better his chances of not having any problems.

"I don't understand," Hector said loudly enough that Jason could hear him. "You are still very young. Why could you not start doing that work now?"

"It takes too much school, too much studying. I'm sick of school, and I'm sick of grades and writing papers and all that crap. If I'm going to do that much work again, I'm gonna get paid for it. I'm not going to pay them to assign me work and then judge it when I turn it in. That doesn't make any sense. Besides, it could all be pretty irrelevant."

"But you already told me that you love to learn. Why could you not learn this job?"

"It's not that easy, Hector," Jason said, not daring to take his eyes off the road. "This storm's great, isn't it?"

"Yes, it is. Why isn't it that easy? You are very good at changing subjects."

"Time, Hector—it takes too much time. Too much time and too much money. I don't have tons of either. And there's no guarantee that I'd even be able to finish a program if I started one. I'd hate to waste that much time and energy on something that I wouldn't even succeed at."

"So you have issues with fear."

"Absotively, my friend. Plenty of issues, plenty of fear. Look at that truck up there—he's having a hard time with this wind and rain."

He pointed to an eighteen-wheeler in the left lane about a quarter of a mile ahead. Its trailer was swaying almost wildly in the wind, and the cab itself was moving back and forth in the lane as if the driver were struggling to maintain control of his vehicle while still trying to maintain his speed.

"Looks like he's got a light load, if any," Jason said. "In this kind of wind, that can be bad news. Don't know what he's doing in the passing lane with that kind of load, though. He should be in the right lane, and going a lot slower than he is."

"It seems that would be the smart thing to do," Hector agreed, his face tense as he watched the trailer swaying in the wind.

"Too many people in too much of a hurry these days," Jason said. "He's gotta be somewhere at a certain time, is my guess. He's not gonna let some stupid storm slow him down when there's a few more dollars to be made." He was keeping his distance behind the truck steady, not wanting to get any closer than he had to. "There he goes," he remarked as the truck moved into the right lane. The highway was fairly crowded with steady traffic, and there were a good six or seven cars between him and the truck, which was still swaying in the wind but not slowing down at all.

"Think I'll just stay back here for a few minutes and see how things go," Jason said to Hector.

"That sounds like a very good idea to me," Hector replied. "I do not know about you, but I am in no special hurry."

"Nope, no hurry here." They both fell silent, listening to the rain pound the roof of the car, watching it cover the windshield between the swipes of the wipers. They watched it splash as it hit the pavement, and they watched the other cars continue to move westward with them. Everything had become blurry, fuzzy, even invisible in the heavy rain, completely different from the way things had been just an hour earlier when the sky had been bright and blue without a single cloud to be seen.

"It is funny to think," Hector said finally, "that the sun is shining right now even though we cannot see it. It is the last thing that we are thinking about when we have such heavy rain, but it is still there shining down on us."

"It sure isn't having much effect," Jason said. "Although I guess that if it wasn't there, this would be a pretty dark rainstorm to be driving through."

"Yes, it would be. This is good during the daytime, but at night I prefer not to be in the rain. Not on the highway. Rainstorms at night are for lying in bed and listening to the rain on the roof, not driving fifty miles an hour on the highway."

"Ahh, you're a romantic, Hector!"

"Yes, I am. An incurable romantic. I shall be romantic until the day I die. I prefer to live life on my own terms. It is the only life I get, so I must live it as I see fit, not as others wish me to. That is something very important that I learned from Leigh."

"I wish I had someone like Leigh in my life," Jason said, both hands still gripping the steering wheel and his eyes still fixed on the road. "Somehow or another, I always run into people like her father. That truck's still all over the place, isn't it?" They had come closer to it in the last few minutes, and they were now following it by some forty yards.

"I think that you were right—the trailer must be empty. That is the only way that it could be moving so much in the wind."

"Well, if you look closely, you can see that there's a line of light on the horizon, which means that we should be coming out of this weather pretty soon. If he can make it a few more minutes, he should be okay. I just don't want to try to pass him when he's swaying so much."

He had barely finished speaking when the cab of the truck jerked suddenly to the left, into the left lane and into the side of a compact car that had been trying to pass it.

"Damn!" Jason yelled, and he instinctively steered to the right as the truck in front of him moved even further to the left. He quickly downshifted and pushed down on the gas pedal, accelerating quickly and flying past the truck just before the trailer started to slide out to the right. For a split second Jason was sure that the trailer was going to smash into his car, but before that could happen, they were past it. Hector turned to look out the back window and Jason watched through the rearview mirror as the trailer seemed to slide sideways in slow motion towards them, the wheels sliding on the wet pavement as if it were ice. The compact car was rolling to the left, off the highway and onto the median, and suddenly the wheels of the trailer finally found traction on the pavement and the entire trailer started to topple over, taking the cab with it.

"Oh my God," Jason said quietly, not daring to stop until he knew they were safely out of reach of the wreck. Finally he did slow, then he stopped in the breakdown lane, and he and Hector looked back at the wreckage behind them. The rain still pounded steadily on the roof, and neither one of them said a word for several moments that seemed to take forever.

Chapter Six

"We must go help," Hector said quietly, opening his door.

"I don't know," Jason replied, his voice a mixture of awe and fear. "I'm not a doctor. Are you?"

"That does not matter," Hector said. "If there are people in need, there must be people who are willing to help. Even if it's only to help to lift a vehicle or to talk to an injured person to keep them calm. There is plenty that one can do, even if one cannot give medical aid." With that, he stepped out of his door into the wind and the rain, instantly becoming soaking wet, and started back towards the wreckage.

"Damn it," Jason muttered, turning the key and killing the engine. He wished for his cell phone, if only to delay him a minute or two while he called 911. He was afraid of what he might find, afraid he might not be able to handle seeing some of the injuries that the accident might have caused. What could he possibly offer to any of the victims? He was sure there had to be people back there who were much more qualified to give help than he was. He pushed his door open and stepped out into the rain, an unenthusiastic volunteer. He ran after Hector.

The tractor trailer looked larger than life on its side, much larger than it had looked through the car's rear window. Even though it was crushed and bent, it still looked huge. To Jason the scene was surreal and unbelievable, for nothing was as it should be. He and Hector should not be able to walk down the middle of an Interstate highway. The red minivan should not be lying on its roof in the median, and the compact car should not be crushed like that, lying on its side. The cars on the other side of the highway should not be slowing and coming to a stop as people jumped out to come and try to help others. There shouldn't be that much screaming in his ears. As they neared the cab of the eighteen-wheeler, Jason saw a face through the broken windshield. It was the face of a burly man with a heavy beard, and the eyes were open wide, either in terror or surprise. It didn't matter which one, because either would have had the same effect. As they came closer, Jason noticed that the eyes weren't blinking at all. He was pretty sure that he was looking at a dead man.

"Oh, shit," he muttered, unable to take his eyes off those of the driver. Hector looked over at him, then reached over and grabbed his chin and turned his head to the left, towards the trees of the forest that lined the highway at that point.

"I believe he is dead," Hector said. "I will check. You may want to help the others who are trying to help those in the van." His words brought Jason back to reality, and he looked over to where Hector was pointing. There were now three or four people around the minivan, and he could hear someone yelling at someone else to stay still. He looked back at the highway behind the truck and saw at least a half-mile of pile-up in the heavy rain, a series of rear-end collisions and fender benders that seemed to be relatively minor, considering the possibilities.

He was soaked through already, and he made his way over to the van. A man in his fifties was lying on the ground near a window, talking to someone inside. Another man just a little older than Jason was looking through the windshield as if trying to figure something out.

"Is there anything I can do to help?" Jason asked. The man looked at him and shook his head, his eyes as dark as the sky.

"I'm not sure," he said in a deep, rough voice that didn't seem to fit his slight build. He was about six feet tall and wore wire-rimmed glasses that seemed pretty useless in the heavy rain—they were covered with water. He took them off and looked at Jason. "I don't know what we should do. I'd like to turn this van back over onto its wheels, but there's a good chance we'd be hurting the survivors inside if we did so. If someone in there has a broken neck or back or something going through them, moving the van may kill them."

"Damn," Jason said, never having thought of that possibility. To him, the obvious course of action would have been to turn the van back over as quickly as possible.

The man on the ground got up. He was in his late 50's, Jason guessed, and just like everyone else his hair was plastered to his head and he was soaked to the skin. He approached Jason and the other man, and a woman who had been looking in the windows also joined them. "Look," he said, "I think it's pretty bad in there. There's a little girl on this side, and she says her brother isn't moving at all.

The driver's unconscious, too, and so is the passenger—
looks like the husband's the driver and the wife is in the
passenger seat.   The little girl is in a child safety seat, so
she had the most protection. It looks like the woman losing
a lot of blood, and I can't reach her with the vehicle upside-
down. I hate to say it, but I think we need to turn this thing
over."

"Don't you think we should wait for the police or
paramedics to make that call?"

"Normally, yes. But she could die while we're waiting for
someone to get here. We're a good twenty or thirty minutes
from anywhere, and anyone who shows up here is going to
be overwhelmed immediately. Look, I'm a doctor. I've
spent a lot of hours in emergency rooms. I'm pretty sure
this is what we need to do."

"Pretty sure, but not positive?" the other man asked.

"Son," the doctor told him, "there's never any 'positive'
in a situation like this. But if we waste more time, we may
lose people that we don't have to lose."

The other man looked at Jason and the woman. "Let's
get it done, then," he said. They all looked behind them
towards the other cars, and they started motioning for
others to join them. In moments they were lined up on one
side of the van, looking for places to get a grip. The doctor
stood apart from them and addressed the whole group over
the sound of the wind and the rain.

"We can't let it slam to the ground once we get it over,"
he yelled. "We need people on the other side to ease it
down gently. We'll also need people at the front and back to
try to control it. Once we get it past its point of balance,
we've hit the pint of no return, and it's going to try to fall
quickly. The people on the end need to try to keep it from
starting down too fast." As he spoke, more people came
over and positioned themselves around the van. In the
distance, the sound of the first siren made its way through
the rain.

"Highway patrol," someone said, recognizing the siren.

"Is everyone ready?" the doctor yelled, and then said,
"Let's go, then!"

Jason lifted with all his might, his feet slipping in the wet
grass. He was amazed to feel the van lifting as if it had no
weight at all. All of their strength together was more than

enough to lift the vehicle, and he didn't need to use nearly as much strength as he was.

"Not too fast," the doctor yelled, and the van seemed to teeter on what used to be two tires, then started to fall slowly as everyone did their best to control its fall. Jason grabbed what used to be a luggage rack and pulled—he knew his effort wouldn't be much, but every little bit had to help, and he felt the lightness of the van that was in so many hands. In a matter of seconds, the van was settled on its wheels. All of the windows were broken out, and Jason looked inside to see a young boy about eight years old sprawled on the seat before him, still in his seatbelt, blood covering his face. He fought the urge to reach in through what used to be a window to touch the boy's neck and search for a pulse; he had no idea what he would do if he couldn't find one. He looked over at the doctor, who was already examining the woman in the passenger seat through the smashed windshield.

He looked back at the boy, then looked up to see the little girl who was in the safety seat next to her brother. How could he have missed her before? She was silent, and her eyes were wide with fear. She had to be about four, and her blond hair was hanging down in her eyes, but she didn't seem to notice it. Their eyes met, and he felt her gaze pierce him to the bottom of his soul. At that moment, the rest of the world vanished. It was just him and this girl here, and in her eyes he saw all of the pain and fear and all of the questioning that he had felt his entire life. In her gaze was the fear of her circumstances, but there was also the light of life, of hope, of possibility. In one instant, he felt that he knew that little girl better than he had ever known anyone else; he felt a connection to her that he had never felt before. She was open to him, she was hiding nothing at all, and that frightened him, confused him, elated him. In the depth of her eyes he saw another human being, another spirit, another person who loved and was here to be loved. And she needed his help.

He knew that he should respond, for the fear in her eyes was crying out to him for some kind of help, some kind of comfort. He wanted to sit down next to her and calm her, but somehow he didn't feel that he could do that. He saw that the top of the van on the other side had smashed down completely, obliterating the window, so his was the only side she could be reached from.

He turned and saw the woman from earlier standing near him.

"Ma'am?" he asked loudly, motioning her over. She stepped over, her eyes questioning. Jason just pointed to the little girl. The woman's face instantly filled with hurt and compassion, and she seemed to forget that Jason was there as she moved closer to the girl and noticed the boy for the first time. Without hesitation, the woman started talking to the girl, and she reached in and pushed the girl's hair out of her eyes. Jason couldn't hear what she was saying.

"Is there another doctor here?" Jason yelled, and a woman who was approaching the van raised her hand slightly. She came over to Jason, and he motioned to the little boy. "I don't know how he is," he told her, then stepped back as she leaned in the window next to the other woman.

Jason suddenly didn't want to know how the boy was. He didn't think he could handle it right then if the boy were dead, so he walked back to the road to look for Hector. He slipped a few times on the wet grass before he reached the pavement, and then he stopped and stared at the scene before him. The highway had been more crowded than he had thought, and the number of cars that were involved in the accident was much greater than he would have imagined. He looked over at the Highway Patrol vehicle that had come to a stop next to the truck, and he watched the trooper standing in the rain talking on the radio. He could only imagine what he was saying. For just a second, he wondered why the trooper wasn't helping anyone, then his logic kicked in and told him that the man had to make sure that others knew just how bad things were. They were going to need a lot of help—a lot of tow trucks, ambulances, paramedics. Even as that thought came to him, he heard another siren in the distance, then it seemed that another joined it, then another.

He turned around and faced the pileup again. How many stories were out there, he wondered—what were these people going through right now, especially those who were hurt and afraid? What were these people going to do now? They wouldn't be getting to where they had been gong for quite a long time now. People would be waiting, wondering why they were late, worrying about them. This sort of thing must have been much worse before there were cell phones, he suddenly thought. At least now people could call others and let them know what had happened, let them know that they were okay.

He found it hard to think. He looked over at the red van and saw the two doctors kneeling over the figure of the little boy, who was now lying on the ground. But his mind wouldn't stay there long enough for him to think anything through. His eyes jumped of their own accord to the trailer that lay crushed and broken on the asphalt, and he was suddenly grateful that the driver hadn't been pulling anything that could have blown up and killed them all. But then the accident probably wouldn't have happened, as the trailer would have been heavier and the wind wouldn't have been able to affect it as much.

"What the hell am I thinking that for?" he asked himself aloud, surprised at the sound of his own voice. The rain was still coming down heavily—if they had been able to continue driving, they probably would have reached the western limit of the storm by then. And where was Hector? He looked all about himself, at the people milling by their cars, many seeming to be in shock or injured, not knowing what to do or whom to help. That was the way he felt—whom could he help? What could he offer?

"Hector!" he yelled out, still scanning the scene for any sign of his passenger. "Hey, Hector!"

"I am here!" Hector yelled back, and Jason saw him waving from next to a white SUV. Hector turned back to the person he had been talking to, and Jason turned around as the vehicles with the sirens finally arrived on the scene. He watched as an ambulance and another emergency vehicle came to a stop by the truck, and the trooper who had been on the radio ran over to them. He pointed to the cab of the truck, and then he pointed to the van and the compact car that somehow Jason hadn't thought at all about going to. The EMT's quickly started pulling boxes from the cabinets on the side of their truck and then moved out to start doing their jobs.

Behind their trucks, a line of flashing lights was approaching, heading east on the westbound lanes. What the hell, Jason thought, there sure wasn't any reason not to. No one was going to be using that road for a while.

"This is very bad," Hector said loudly next to him, and Jason jumped. "Many people are hurt and will have to go to the hospitals."

"Yeah," Jason said. "I know."

Hector looked at him carefully, peering at him closely. "I think now would be a good time to go on," he said. "There is nothing more that we can contribute here."

"You mean leave? Are we allowed to do that? What if they want to ask us questions or something like that? We are witnesses."

Hector shrugged. "If they need answers, they have many witnesses. There is nothing that many people here have not seen. And I believe that you are in shock now. It would be good for us to get into some dry clothes and get some coffee, perhaps. We can serve no other purpose here but to get in the way. The paramedics and the police are here, and they have much work to do. We cannot help them with it."

"I suppose you're right," Jason said. "I'd just feel weird leaving."

"As will I, *mijo*. But if we stay, we are in the way and contributing nothing. Our time for helping is past, and we did what we needed to do. Now it is time for others to take over."

Jason sighed. He didn't want to leave, and he wanted nothing more than to leave and be on the road again. He still felt torn, and it wasn't until Hector put a hand on his shoulder and started to lead him back to his car that he was actually able to start to move one way or another.

"By the way," Hector said as they walked past the trailer, "I must thank you for saving my life."

"Huh?" Jason asked, puzzled. "What are you talking about?"

"Your reflexes are very good. If you had not been able to get around the truck as you did, then we would have crashed into the truck. I am sure of that. You would not have been able to stop the car on the wet road."

"Yeah, but that's just driving. Anyone could have done that."

"No." Hector shook his head. "Most people would have tried to stop the car. They would have stepped on the brakes reflexively, and they would have ended up crashing into the truck. I am alive now because of your ability to drive. Thank you."

Jason was perplexed. "I really didn't do anything, though."

Hector smiled, a sad smile. "I have found that the easiest thing to say when someone thanks me is 'You're welcome.' It is simple and quick and very appropriate."

"Okay. You're welcome. I guess."

"Good. And we also are the only people who will be able to drive away now, also due to your driving skill. We will be able to go somewhere and change into dry clothes."

"Oh, man—this is gonna suck, getting into the car all soaked like this. We're gonna get the seats soaked, and when we change clothes we're just gonna sit in the wet seats and get soaked again." He turned and looked behind them at what was now a sea of emergency vehicles with their lights flashing in the rain, with even more speeding past them as they continued walking. "Still, I guess a little water isn't going to hurt us. Things could be a lot worse, couldn't they?"

"Things for us could be very, very bad. I am very grateful that they are not."

"You and me both."

"Will you be okay to drive?" Hector asked him. "You seem to be very deep in a place that may not be good for driving."

"I'll be okay," Jason assured him. "Once I get behind the wheel, I'm back where I need to be. I'm always focused when I drive. Maybe that's why I love it so much."

Hector didn't answer, and they both got into the car. Jason started it up and started slowly westward on the empty road, turning on his emergency blinkers so that any vehicles coming the wrong way down the highway would be able to see his car. They slowly distanced themselves from the chaos behind them.

"I feel kind of guilty, leaving like this," Jason said.

"And what are our options?" Hector asked simply. "We would stand there doing nothing for a very long time until someone found the time to talk to us, and they would learn nothing from us that they hadn't heard from many other people. We all wish to help, but it is important to know also when our help no longer is needed. Some things were meant for other people to take care of. People trained to do it."

"I guess you're right. . . . still. . . ." Jason's voice trailed off as he realized that he had nothing more to say. "Isn't there some sort of law about leaving the scene of an accident?"

"Yes, but I believe only if you were involved in it. We were not involved—we only stopped to help. It is interesting—forty-five minutes ago, you did not want to stop at all. Now you do not want to leave."

"Forty-five minutes? You've got to be kidding." He looked at the clock on the stereo, and he shook his head. "Man, that seemed more like five minutes. That's just crazy."

"Yes," Hector agreed, "time always is crazy. It always is relative, and even though it passes at the same rate always, it seems to pass more slowly or more quickly depending on what we are doing."

"I guess so," Jason said quietly, showing no interest in continuing the conversation. Suddenly his mind was back on the little girl in the van.

Hector peered ahead through the rain, which was finally starting to weaken. "It looks like there is an exit ahead. Perhaps we could change into some dry clothes."

"That would be a good idea," Jason said, not taking his eyes off the road. He wondered how the little girl was doing right then, and how her family was. He found himself hoping fervently that her mother and father and brother were alright, that they would recover completely. He hoped that what he had seen had been deceptive—that their lack of movement and their seeming lack of life had been due to unconsciousness. He knew that he hadn't even looked at the boy long enough to see if he was breathing or not, so there definitely was hope that he was alive.

But he also knew that the roof of the van was at least a foot lower than it should have been, and the force necessary for that to happen could easily have killed anyone whose head hit the roof as it collapsed.

The exit led to another cookie-cutter gas station, complete with a convenience store and all the trappings of all the other places that looked exactly like it. Hector had pulled dry clothes out of the bag that he had put at his feet, and he started for the restroom.

"I will change first," he told Jason. "I will be quick."

"Okay," Jason said, almost not hearing what he had said. He went to the trunk of his car and opened the suitcase that lay on top of everything else, pulling out a complete change of clothes. He hated to have to take off his most comfortable pair of jeans, but there wasn't much he could do about it. He also pulled out a towel from a different bag to put over his seat, and after thinking about it for a moment, he got a second one for Hector. Then he tossed the two towels onto the seats and went inside the store.

"How ya doin'?" the attendant asked him enthusiastically. He was in his thirties, a short man with wire-rimmed glasses and floppy blond hair, but no name tag. "It's about time this rain let up, isn't it?" he asked.

"Huh?" Jason asked, then came back down to earth. "Oh, yeah—I guess so. A real good thing."

"You guys heading east?" the man asked. "Sounds like there's a pretty big pileup about fifteen miles down the road. We haven't had any cars heading west for quite a while now. It's kind of spooky."

Jason almost told him where they had just been, then thought better of it. He didn't feel like talking about it. "Yeah, we're heading east. Is it tying traffic up?"

"Nah—there's just a pretty big slow-down, I think, but people are getting through. It's just the west-bound traffic that's messed up."

Hector came out of the bathroom just then, barefoot and carrying his soaked clothing, and Jason took his chance to avoid more conversation. "I'm soaked," he told the man. "You don't mind if I change in the restroom, do you?"

"Not at all," the man replied. "I'd appreciate it if you'd dry things up after yourself, though. There's plenty of paper towels in there."

"Thanks. I'll do that." He went into the bathroom and closed the door behind him.

Suddenly, he was alone. It was a feeling he hadn't expected, but it was the strongest sense of aloneness he ever had felt. He felt tears welling up inside him suddenly and forcefully, and before he knew it, he was sobbing quietly and his arms and legs began to shake. He sat down on the floor, unable to stand any longer, and he buried his face in the crook of his arm.

It didn't last long—just about a minute. The whole time, though, the little girl's eyes were with him, there in his mind. He felt her helplessness, felt her fear, felt her need for someone to do something for her. Just as strongly he felt his own helplessness in the face of being needed, felt his own need to have someone take from him the responsibility that had been thrust upon him simply by the fact that he had been standing where he was.

When his sobbing subsided, he took a deep breath and held it for a few moments, then let it out slowly. He stood, taking off his shoes, then his shirt and his pants. He wanted to make himself busy so that he had something else to think about, and changing his clothes was the only other thing he had to do at the moment. He regretted having left the towels in the car, and he ended up having to use his socks and paper towels to dry himself off as much as he could. He wasn't going to wear the socks anyway—his shoes were completely soaked, and there was no use trying to put them on again. In just a couple of minutes he had changed clothes and cleaned up, and he took another deep breath and left the bathroom.

Hector spied him from across the room. "Would you like some coffee, *amigo*?" he called over to him. The cashier was busy with a customer.

"That would be great," Jason said, approaching Hector. "I could really use a jolt of something right about now. Might as well be caffeine."

"Hector handed him a cup of coffee. "It is decaffeinated. It is better for you." He looked Jason in the eyes, and then he smiled. "I am only joking, my friend. It is regular coffee. French roast. Though I do not know why so many companies that make coffee think that the French know something special about roasting coffee. There are many types of coffee that taste much better than the French roast."

Jason somehow felt uncomfortable, and he didn't know why. It didn't seem right to him that they could be talking so. . . . *normally* after what they had just experienced. Somehow it seemed to be disrespectful to be talking about coffee when the people they had just left were dealing with death and destroyed vehicles and injuries. He and Hector had just driven away, unharmed and unscathed. There was something absurd about the fact that they were completely okay, while the lives of so many others had just been changed so drastically forever. And they had been there, right in the middle of it all. Where would they be if he hadn't been so close to the tractor-trailer when it went out of control? What would they be doing right now? He was pretty sure that they wouldn't be talking about French roast coffee.

"It is very difficult, is it not?" Hector asked him, looking him straight in the eyes. "Now much of the world seems petty, as if it does not matter a bit. Nothing seems to be important at all, because we have just seen something that puts all of life into a different perspective. What has been important always no longer is important. But with time, you will find that everything will return to normal. Life goes on, *mi amigo*, and we go with it."

Jason shook his head. "It doesn't seem right. That little girl didn't do anything to anyone, and look at her. She might have lost both of her parents and her brother, and for what? What did she do to deserve that?"

"Deserve?" Hector sounded surprised. "You are assuming that someone caused that to happen in order to hurt someone else, if you talk about someone *deserving* something like that. Sometimes terrible things just happen, and people are caught in the middle of them whether they want to be there or not. Do victims of an earthquake deserve to be victims? Nobody wants it, but in life things happen. We have to take what comes our way sometimes, but that does not mean that we *deserve* what happens to us."

"But what possible purpose could something like that serve? What good can come from this?"

Hector actually smiled—it wasn't a smile of humor, but Jason couldn't figure out what was behind it. "What do we know of the future?" he asked. "It is possible that this little girl is going to grow up as an orphan, living with her grandparents who love her very dearly, and she may one day write an important book that will help many other people in ways that we cannot know. Perhaps it will be a book about growing up without parents. Perhaps it will be about dealing with loss. Perhaps it will be a funny novel that will allow people to see many things in life in different ways. We cannot know."

"But you don't know that's going to happen."

"Of course not. Perhaps she will see herself as a victim and close herself up, becoming very lonely and depressed and kill herself when she is a teenager. I do not know. But it is the not knowing that allows me to accept the truth that many things are possible as results of this situation, and not all of them are bad. There will be pain, and there will be loss, but the human spirit is a very resilient thing. When we think about how awful things are, we are not giving people the credit that they deserve for being able to overcome many things and to thrive when they do so."

Jason sighed. "I guess you're right." They started walking towards the cashier, carrying their wet clothes in one hand and their coffees in the other.

"All set there?" the cashier asked cheerfully. "I hope you guys don't get slowed down too much when you pass the pileup."

"We'll be okay," Jason assured him.

"That'll be two dollars and fifty-three cents," the cashier said, reaching out and taking the wet five-dollar bill that Jason handed to him. "I guess I'll let this one sit out and dry for a while," he said with a smile.

"Thanks," Jason said, putting his change in his pocket and picking up his coffee. "And have a good day."

"Thanks—you, too. And drive carefully. The roads should be better now that the rain's let up, but you never know."

"You're right there," Jason said. "You never know." They went to the door and out into the sunshine. The sky before them was still dark with heavy rain clouds, but the sky above was bright blue. He and Hector walked out to his car.

"It is our connection with other people that causes us to feel," Hector said. "If we had read about this accident in the paper, we would not have the strong feelings that we now have. You would not have seen the little girl in a moment of great vulnerability, and you would not have felt the compassion that you feel so strongly."

Jason sighed once more. He knew that Hector was right, and that there was nothing he could do about anything anymore. "Looks like it'll be a nice drive from here on in," he said. "I don't know what I'm gonna do with these, though." He held up his wet clothes. "I wish there were some way we could dry them."

"We could attach them to the antenna," Hector said.

Jason laughed. "That would be quite the sight, wouldn't it? Maybe I could turn on the heater and we could put them on the floor. That would dry them out, but it would get really hot in the car."

"We could open the windows in back and put the clothes on the back seat. The wind would dry them. There are many possibilities."

"Not that many, Hector. And none of them sound very practical. I guess putting them on the back seat is the best idea, but it's gonna be pretty loud driving at seventy with the windows wide open." He opened one of the back doors and rolled down the window, then laid out his shirt and pants on the back of the seat. Hector did the same on his side.

"That is okay—the noise can keep us awake. You should be getting tired pretty soon, no?"

Jason sighed. "I figured I would, but after that, I don't think I'm going to be sleepy any time soon. Too much going on in my head that I can't slow down, can't get rid of. I keep seeing that girl's face, and I keep thinking I should have done more for her."

"Then you probably will be thinking of her for a very long time, until you are ready to give yourself credit for the fact that you did all you could. You helped her in the best way that you were able at that particular time. You are who you are and you are able to do what you are able to do. You are not trained in medicine or emergency situations. You did the best that you could. Now you must move on and keep living your life. She will be with you forever, and I hope that you do not see her as a reminder of some sort of failure. Let her be a reminder to you of your compassion, of your desire to help others, a reminder of the fact that we all need help from others sometimes, and we all can be called to help others at any time."

"How'd you get to be so wise, old man? That doesn't bother you, does it, if I call you old man? It just seems to fit."

Hector shrugged. "I am old. You are young. It is natural that you look up to me with respect and admiration." He laughed. "I am not particularly wise, though. I just try to pay attention when life teaches me its lessons. And then

I try to pass them on to others. It is the teacher in my blood."

"Well, you seem to be a pretty good teacher."

"Thank you."

"No problem. I just hope that someday I turn out to be a good student and actually learn something that does me some good in life."

Hector laughed. "You already have learned much in life, *mijo*. But most of what you have learned is inside of you, waiting to come out, waiting to be used. Until you are ready to use it, it will stay inside of you. When you are ready, you will find that it is already there. You will know how to use it when it is time."

"I hope you're right."

"Of course I am right. I am a wise old man, no?"

"I hope you're not going to make me regret having said that. . . ."

Chapter Seven

Jason felt better after having stopped, and he rolled his own window all the way down as they took off. The blue sky and the fresh air energized him, and he felt more awake and more alive than he had twenty minutes before. He even felt a bit surprised at himself for feeling so good after having seen what he had just seen. Maybe Hector's words had helped him—maybe it was true that life does go on, no matter what.

"I don't see how cops and paramedics and firemen and doctors can do it," he said once they were back on the highway. The westbound lanes were still almost completely empty, a fact that kept the accident foremost in his thoughts.

"What is that?" Hector asked.

"Do that. See stuff like that accident all the freakin' time, but still be able to lead their normal lives. I think it would drive me crazy, to be honest."

"That is why you do not feel called to do that type of work. People are usually able to rise up to the levels they need to reach in order to survive and to maintain their sanity. I have known many people who have gone to war, but who have come back and still have been able to be happy people. I can only imagine the things that they have seen in war, and I do not imagine pretty things. But they learn how to cope, most of them. Not all of them. Many people carry the images and experiences with them for the rest of their lives, and they allow them to control their lives and the way they live."

Jason looked over at him. "What do you mean, 'allow them to control'? We're in control of ourselves. Aren't we?"

Hector laughed. "That is one of the great myths of the world. Very few people are in control of themselves. Most people are controlled by their own thoughts, and most people never have learned how to control their thoughts, how to quiet their minds. This is something that I learned from a man who taught philosophy, but not the kind of philosophy you might think. He was the only philosophy teacher I knew who taught people to think for themselves, instead of always saying 'Kant said this,' or 'Socrates said that.' He wanted his students to develop their own philosophies of life, and he always said that his job was to plant seeds that would allow them to do that."

"But our thoughts are our own. We control them, don't we—we can choose what we want to think of."

"Yes, but most people do not do so. Most people allow their thoughts to control their moods and emotions, as if they were grass on the plains that is being blown about by the wind. The wind makes the grass bend as it blows, and the grass cannot choose not to bend in certain directions. Most people focus their minds on whatever enters, no matter how destructive or negative or even untrue it can be. Advertisers and marketers depend on us not being able to control our thoughts in order to sell us things and make us want to buy certain brand names. He helped me to see that for example, during my angry years I focused almost exclusively on thoughts and ideas that would keep me angry. When a thought would come like 'My mother is a wonderful woman who deserves my love,' I always would think, 'Yes, but. . . .' and then come up with reasons for which I still should be mad at her. She did not deserve my anger, but I still was angry. That was because I always let the angry thoughts be the stronger thoughts. I use those memories now to help me to keep my mind on more positive things. I always ask myself whether a thought will help me to contribute to the positive part of the world, or if it will cause me to contribute to the darker side."

Jason was silent for several long moments after Hector finished speaking. "I think I do that, too," he said finally. Hector waited patiently for him to continue. "I get depressed sometimes, and one thing I always notice is that I just dismiss any thoughts that don't help the depression to stay strong. I tell myself, 'You shouldn't feel this way,' and then I immediately tell myself that I'm wrong, that of course I should feel that way, because my life sucks and everything is awful, that nobody loves me, that no one cares if I'm happy or depressed, if I live or die—all that crap. I hate being depressed, but it's like when I am depressed, I want to stay there and not feel better, no matter what."

"My sister used to get depressed very often. Does it happen much to you?"

Jason thought it over. "Every once in a while," he said. "I don't know if there's something that causes it or triggers it, but I'll just start feeling like I'm sliding down this huge slide, but I'm not completely aware of it. I'll start feeling bad, and it's like the bad feelings start feeding on themselves and on each other and grow and bring in more bad thoughts. I get to the point where I can't see anything bright in the world, and even though I want to break out of it, I can't. Is that how it was with your sister?"

Hector shrugged. "I think so. She did not talk about it much. In those days, people did not share their feelings nearly as much as people do now. Many people exaggerate this and tell too much, but I believe that it is a good thing that people are more willing to talk about what is hurting them. That is the only way that we can get help, after all— to let others know that we need it. And that is the only way that we can help others—by knowing what it is that they need help with." He stopped speaking and put his hand out the window into the air stream that was flowing around the car. He smiled. "This wind is going seventy miles an hour," he said, "and it does not even exist if this car does not drive down the road as it is doing now. It is amazing, no?"

"Yeah. Truly amazing. So how does your sister deal with her depression?"

Hector sighed. "When we were younger, she would find a place to hide and cry. When we had our own rooms after my mother married again, she would stay in her room and cry. When she was twenty-five, I think, she killed herself."

He said it so matter-of-factly that Jason was startled. "Oh, my God," he said. "I'm sorry—I didn't know."

"Of course you did not know. I had not told you. She was about to be married, and she was in her second year of teaching elementary school. She taught second-graders, and she was very good with them. She had an apartment of her own, and one day in the middle of summer she took many, many sleeping pills. She was the kind of person who would not want to leave a mess for other people to clean up, so she could not have shot herself or hurt herself in another way. A friend of hers found her body when she went to her apartment to go for a walk with her. They went for a long walk every evening during the summer."

"That must have been very hard for you."

"It was very hard for everyone, but of course it was the hardest for my mother. She grieved for many months, and she wore only black the entire time. She grieved until Thanksgiving day, I remember, and on that day she wore her favorite red dress. It must have been the idea of being grateful for all that we have in life that allowed her to abandon her grieving. I was glad that she gave it up, for such a thing easily can become too important a part of a person. I think the hardest part for all of us was that my sister did not leave a note. She did not say good-bye, so all of us always have felt that there is something missing in our relationships with her. She left for ever, yet we did not have the opportunity to say good-bye."

"I've thought about suicide a few times," Jason said quietly, "but only when I'm depressed. And even then I don't feel like it's me thinking about it—it's not something that makes sense to me, if you know what I mean."

"Well, I for one am very glad that you never have gone through with it. That would have been a great tragedy."

Jason laughed. "Yeah, then you might not have gotten a ride to Pocatello." He knew as soon as he said it that it wasn't funny, but the words came out all on their own.

Hector looked at him long and hard. "You should not say such things," he told Jason. "Even if you feel you are joking, such things are not funny. Do not belittle yourself. Our lives should be about building ourselves and others up, not about tearing down."

"Sorry," Jason muttered. "It's just an old habit. It's kind of hard to build yourself up when nobody's ever taught you how."

"What do you mean?"

"It's just that—" he paused, thinking, sounding almost as if he didn't want to say any more, or couldn't. "It's just that I'm not used to looking at the positive side of myself because no one else ever did. I always learned to look at the negative sides of myself. Hell, I never used to think there were any positive sides."

"Did your parents criticize you often when you were young?"

"I don't know if criticize is the right word. They always seemed to be disappointed in me. It was like I couldn't do anything right, so I gave up even trying. And once I gave up—well, that was it. I didn't have any chance anymore. I always used to think that my brother had it made, that he couldn't do anything wrong and I couldn't do anything right. We didn't have any sibling rivalry or anything like that, but my parents never seemed to be disappointed in him.

Everything he did was golden, while everything that I did was flawed. He did great in school, I was average or below average. He was great at sports, while I didn't really like sports much. He always dated the prettiest girls in high school, while I—hell, I didn't show any interest in dating at all. He was a chip off the old block, and I was the black sheep." He laughed softly. "Those are two completely worn-out clichés, don't you think?"

Hector shrugged. "If the words carry the message that you wish them to carry, then the words are valuable to you and your story. Do not be so judgmental of yourself for your choice of words."

"Yeah, whatever. In any case, how did we get on that depressing stuff? Can't we talk about something cheerful? Haven't we been through enough negative stuff today?"

"Possibly. Or perhaps not enough. Much of our strength comes from the bottoms of the valleys that we walk through, and we never will be as strong as we can be if we do not visit the valleys."

"That's a fine theory, I guess, but I much prefer the mountaintops. I've been in far too many valleys for my personal taste. Give me the sunshine and a nice strong wind on top of a mountain any day."

"Yes, the mountaintop is more exhilarating, but the valleys hold the secrets to ourselves, the sides of ourselves that we will not find on top of the mountain, and the sides that if we do not know them, can come to hurt us one day, even more than if we never had gotten to know them. What have you learned more from—the trials that you have passed through, or the times that you have spent feeling wonderful?"

Jason considered the question. "The trials, I guess. I like feeling good, but I don't usually learn a whole lot when I do. At least not as much as when I'm going through something difficult."

"I believe that most people would answer the same way."

"I can buy that."

"Then we must ask ourselves why we spend so much of our time trying to avoid going through trials. If they are going to teach us more about ourselves than the good times, then why do we try to make the good times last forever and avoid the trials? Shouldn't we seek out the trials in order to grow as human beings?"

"That sounds good, but you wouldn't catch me seeking them out. I'd be too afraid that I wouldn't make it through them. Like I wouldn't start running a marathon because I know that I'd never be able to finish it. I don't want any trials that could bring me down so far that I might not make it through them."

"Yet if you wish to run a marathon, you could train and put yourself through many smaller trials to be able to make it through the great one. But so it is with life. Because of our fears, we spend much time and energy avoiding the things that can make us stronger people. We avoid the things that could help us to learn to help others. We look for comfort and safety, and we try to make such fleeting things permanent. It is truly interesting. We can climb mountains for fun and enjoyment, yet avoid talking to neighbors because they might hurt us. We can marry someone because we love them, but then keep them away with walls that we build because we're afraid that if we allow them to get too close, they will hurt us by leaving us. And then—" Hector laughed—"and then they leave us because we have kept them from passing through those very walls. We are a very ironic race, I believe."

"Yeah, and a lot of what we do doesn't make sense. Why do you think that is?"

"I do not know. Why do people concern themselves with your sexuality? We say that sexuality is a private matter, but if your sexuality does not fit in with what we think is right, then we cast you out. Why were people so concerned that I was Mexican, that my parents were born in Mexico? Do you know that many people think that a person is more likely to steal if that person is Mexican? Or black? There are many, many people who are neither Mexican nor black who steal, but these people do not think that white people are likely to steal. If a Mexican steals, it validates their prejudice. If a white person steals, it surprises them very much. But it should not—people steal, not races. And in many cultures people have different ideas of what it means to own something, so people from these cultures are more likely to take something that does not belong to them—we would call this stealing, but they would not. We define our own realities and we grow comfortable within them, and then we try to see the world in ways that fit our visions of reality. And if what you do violates the way that I see reality, then what you do must be wrong. That is one of the main reasons that many people use religion—to help them define their realities and to judge those who do not fit into them. Religions are very good for this, for they always have many rules and doctrines already set up for you to adopt as your own. And once you do, your reality is defined for you."

"Wow—I never thought of it that way."

"You will, one day. When you are old, like me, and you have lived more of your life. You will start to see the ways that people try to make their own worlds easier to live in. I do not try to control my world, though—I try to live in it and accept it for what it is, and make the most of all that is in my world. This is a great lesson that children teach us—look at the world with wonder and awe and accept what it gives you without judging what it gives you, and you will be very rich indeed. Unfortunately, we end up trying to teach children to see the world in our ways instead of learning again to see it their ways, which often is a much healthier way of seeing the world."

"I miss being a kid. Things were so much easier then."

"Possibly. If they were, it was because we had not yet learned how to complicate things as much as we know how to complicate them now." Hector sighed. "Sometimes it is very sad to see what man has made of man. Wordsworth said that. 'Have I not reason to lament what man has made of man?' He was a very observant man. But now I must sleep, I think, because my mind is very tired. It has been a very long morning."

Jason looked at the clock and was shocked to see that it wasn't even one o'clock yet. He was starting to feel tired himself. "There's rest stop coming up in a few miles," he said. "I'll pull in there and we can get some sleep."

Ten minutes later he pulled into the rest area and cruised slowly past the bathrooms towards the end of the parking lot. He parked at the far end, away from everyone. He was looking forward to the sleep, and he was surprised at just how quickly and strongly the sleepiness had come upon him. The last five minutes had been brutal, just trying to keep his eyes open. Rubbing the back of his neck hadn't worked well, nor had shaking his head or even pinching himself. He was thankful that the rest area had been so close; if he had had to drive further to get to one, he wasn't even sure that he would have made it.

Hector was already asleep, curled up with his head against the door. Jason raised both windows until they were cracked open, then closed the rear windows and locked the doors. Then he reclined in his seat and lay back, trying to make himself comfortable. The sleeping in the car was the only part of long road trips that he didn't like, for he found that it was awkward and uncomfortable. He almost never slept well, even for short periods of time. Once the first full night of driving was over, he would sleep just well enough to allow him to stay awake for another six or eight hours, then he would have to pull over again for a few hours more of sleep.

Not long after he closed his eyes, his focus was on the crash and the face of the little girl was there in his mind quite clearly. He could see her eyes, and he could only imagine what her voice would have sounded like had she spoken. I'm sorry I couldn't help you, he said to himself, knowing that she never would know just how sorry he felt.

But was Hector right—had he really done the best thing he could in the circumstances he found himself in? Maybe trying to calm her himself would have been useless, while the woman might have been perfect for the task. Was he beating himself up over nothing? Maybe what he needed was praise for having done the right thing, but praise wasn't something he ever gave lightly to himself.

He tried to breathe deeply, paying attention to his breath so that he could get his mind off the girl. It was a trick his partner had taught him, and one that he had gotten pretty good at. It worked well enough this time to clear his mind so that he could relax a bit and fall asleep. Not a restful and peaceful sleep, but sleep nonetheless, and any sleep was better than none. He woke up twice with a start as he felt his body moving forward—the inertia from so many hours of driving was tricking his mind into thinking that his was a body in motion. Both times it took him several seconds to remember exactly where he was and what he was doing, and both times he was able to fall right back asleep.

He awoke about four in the afternoon. He was groggy and his head felt unclear at first, but he felt the draw of the road once more. He felt that he needed to be driving again, and he wanted to be moving.

Hector wasn't in the car with him. At first he didn't even notice his absence, but he soon realized that something was missing. The passenger door was locked, and for several moments he wondered if Hector had decided to find a ride with someone else, someone more interesting, someone that he'd prefer to spend time with. After all, Jason was sure that he wasn't the best company in the world. Maybe he should have tried to tell more stories about his own life rather than just listening to Hector tell his. He imagined that Hector could see him as being pretty selfish.

But then he noticed Hector's bag still on the floor. He sat up and put his seat back in its upright position. He looked out the windows and he spied Hector sitting on a picnic table, his feet on the bench and his elbows on his thighs, his hands together with the fingers intertwined as he stared off into the distance. Behind the rest area was a large field of grass that easily could have reached to Jason's chest if he were to walk in it, and behind that started a forest. Hector stared in that direction, and Jason imagined him at that moment a dreamer, a poet searching for inspiration or searching for words that would make his inspiration a reality, something tangible.

He got slowly out of the car, knowing that his legs would be worse now than they had been. He had to go to the bathroom, but he wanted to check in with Hector first. He took his first few steps very slowly to get his walking legs back, and then he went over to the picnic table where Hector sat. He sat down, too, not saying a word, and looked out at the grass and the forest.

"Hello, *amigo mío*," Hector said quietly. "You have slept?"

"I have slept," Jason replied. "I slept pretty well, too," he fibbed, not wanting Hector to worry that he might be too sleepy to drive.

"That is good," Hector said, not removing his gaze from the scene before him.

"What are you looking at?" Jason asked after a few long moments.

Hector shrugged. "I do not know," he said. "I am not looking so much as I am thinking. I never have seen this particular field before, or that forest behind it. I am wondering what kind of life there is right before me that I cannot even see. In that grass must live many snakes, insects, birds, perhaps even foxes and mice and other animals. In the forest beyond, how many different creatures are living their lives right at this moment, with no idea at all that I am sitting here watching the edges of their world? And they do not care that I watch. It does not matter to them because it does not affect them. Why are we trained to see only the surfaces of things and people without regard for the life that is deeper than the surface? When we learn to live life that way, we lose the opportunity to see and feel the very essence of life, the very depths of life that we only can guess at because we do not see it."

"Maybe it's too scary for us," Jason said. "Maybe if we were able to see the depths, we'd lose our minds. Go insane."

Hector turned to him slowly and regarded him very curiously. "That is a very wise thing that you say," he told Jason. "I am very impressed with your insight."

"Thanks," Jason said awkwardly, not sure if Hector was being serious or was joking with him.

"You are welcome," Hector replied, turning back around and returning his gaze to the scene before him. "The question is, though: What is so wrong with losing our minds? Just what are we trying to preserve by not losing them?"

Jason laughed. "That's a good question. Sometimes I wonder. Sometimes the people that other people call 'flakes' seem to be much happier than the ones we all call 'normal.' I think sometimes it's good to be weird."

"Personally, I would not be any other way," Hector said. "I want to be weird always, for only in weirdness can we find the normal. We all are trained to see the world in certain ways, and that keeps us from seeing the world as it really is. And we create these carefully controlled façades for ourselves that become so normal that it makes me sick sometimes to see them. In order to become 'normal,' people have sacrificed their sense of play, their ability to have fun, their willingness to try different things and to take risks. It is so very sad."

"I don't play much," Jason said quietly. "It seems that if I play, I lose. The time I spend playing could be time spent getting ahead, and I know so many other people who spend their time getting ahead. So if I don't do the same, I'd be falling so far behind."

"Behind what, *mijo*? Perhaps you wish to be a part of this rat race, but personally I do not feel like racing against other rats. I would much prefer to be flying with the dragons or running with the unicorns. With them, not against them."

"Unicorns? Dragons? Come on Hector—even you have to admit that there's no such thing. Except in your imagination, maybe."

"What is my imagination? It is a very real part of me, is it not?"

"Well, yeah. But what we imagine isn't always real."

"If we imagine it, it is real. Just because other people cannot see it or do not know how to share it does not make it any less real. Have you ever read anything by a man named Pirandello?"

"Never heard of him."

"Most people have not. He wrote a play about characters who had been created by a writer, but then abandoned. The play never was finished, and they were looking for some sort of play that they could exist in. Because once they were created, they *were*. It is a very interesting thought. Once I create a unicorn, it *is*. You do not need to see it in physical form for it to be any more real in my world."

"So you live in a world with unicorns?"

"As do you."

"Sorry Hector—with all due respect, there aren't any unicorns in my world. Unicorns are supposed to be magical and beautiful, and there isn't a whole lot of magic or beauty in my world."

Hector turned to face him. "What are you running from, Jason? What is your story of right now, the story that has put you on the road to Seattle?" His eyes were fixed on Jason's, and his voice was sincere and caring. And curious.

Suddenly Jason felt that things couldn't be real. He couldn't be sitting in a rest area in Illinois with a man he had never met until a few hours before, facing a field full of tall grass on a beautiful afternoon in June. He couldn't be wanting to share such personal information with this man, stuff that was better kept to himself because he knew that no one else gave a damn about it. He had wanted change when he had taken off the previous afternoon, but he never would have guessed that such profound changes could occur in less than twenty-four hours, that he could have been exposed to such new ways of seeing things.

He sighed. He knew that he was going to tell the story, so he figured it would be best to get it told and out in the open.

"About a week ago," he said, "pretty much everything in my world started falling apart. A couple of my best friends left and moved to Florida—they had one winter too many in New England, I guess. Another friend was arrested for possession of cocaine, and they're going to come down on him pretty hard, I think. He had quite a bit on him when they arrested him, so it'll be pretty easy to make an example of him, especially since he was dealing. And of course, this was the time that my partner decided that he had to move on, that it was important for him to end our relationship and start all over. He felt like I was suffocating him, like I wasn't giving him enough room and enough freedom, and he needed to feel free again."

"Were you?" Hector asked quietly.

Jason fought the urge to say "Hell, no!" He knew that the truthful answer to that question was somewhere inside of him, but he didn't know where or what it was. "I don't know," he said. "I didn't think that I was, but I guess it's possible. I've thought about it a lot, but I can't figure it out, to be honest."

"Not all things must be figured out," Hector said simply.

"This all happened when I was in and out of one of my depressions, and I was reaching the point where I couldn't think clearly any more. I spent two whole days in bed, not even eating anything. All I got up for was to go to the bathroom, and I usually drank a glass of water when I did. I wasn't aware of time passing, and I didn't know or care if it was night or day. It was like this immense, heavy fog had settled in over me, and I couldn't see or hear or feel anything clearly. It was one of my worst depressions. And because I didn't show up for work or call in sick or anything, I got fired.

"When the fog started clearing, I started to think that maybe all this was some sort of sign. God or life or the universe or whatever it is that's in charge of life was giving me a pretty clear signal that it was time to move on."

"How did you know that?" Hector asked.

"It was simple—I no longer had anything there that would make me want to stay. I had a few acquaintances, and I probably could have gotten a new job and made some new friends, but when all was said and done there was no reason any more for me not to move. So I decided to move. I went to this guy at a pawnshop and had him come clean out my apartment—all the furniture, the TV, the stereo, everything—and take it with him. I sold it all to him really cheap, but it gave me enough money to move on and make a new start."

"I admire your willingness to take a risk," Hector said.

"Or put my tail between my legs and turn and run."

"I suppose one could see it that way, but I do not believe that you should put yourself in the same category as a cowardly dog."

"Okay, how about a cowardly young twenty-something, then? A cowardly Gen-Xer? I'm not even sure if I'm Generation X or Generation Y."

"That does not matter. Too many people want us to label ourselves and thing of ourselves in certain ways. It helps them to sell their merchandise to us. You are Jason. You are not a coward, and you are not a part of any group just because of the year you were born."

"Thanks. I know you're right. But anyway, I decided on Seattle because I had just read a long article about it, and I figured that if God or the universe was giving me a message about moving on. Maybe putting that article in my hands a few weeks ago was another part of the same message. You know—'It's time to move on, Jason, and here's a pretty cool place you can move to.'"

"That could be true," Hector said. "The older I become, the less I believe in coincidence. I believe now that there are no coincidences. I am very impressed that you are able to see such connections at your age. When I had your age, I would not ever have been able to see such connections in things. To me, everything was exactly what I saw it to be on the surface. It would be many years before I started to see the meaning behind things and within things."

"Well, there's really nothing to be impressed about."

"Do you allow people to compliment you?"

"What do you mean?"

"If you do not allow people to compliment you and say nice things to you, then you are robbing them of the opportunity to make positive contributions to your life. That is very difficult for anyone to deal with, and even harder for people who love you to deal with."

Jason stared at Hector, feeling as if he had been struck in the face with something very heavy and hurtful. He felt breathless, and he felt a strong urge to lash out in self-defense. He also knew, though, that there was nothing to defend himself against.

"You're probably right," he said quietly.

Hector turned back to look at the field. "It may be interesting to you to know that I, too, am running. But I am not running to or from anything. I am simply running against time."

Jason had been about to get up, but Hector's words surprised him. "What do you mean?" he asked.

"I told you earlier that I was going to see my son and his wife and my grand-daughter. I am going because I do not have much time to see them any more. Their house burned down very recently, and all three of them were trapped inside. They did not get out."

Jason was astonished. "So they're in the hospital? Are they going to be alright?"

Hector shook his head. "No. All three of them died. I did not find out about it until yesterday. I missed the funeral, which was two weeks ago."

"Then. . . . I don't understand. How are you racing against time?"

"I wish to see them in the cemetery while I still am able to understand where I am and what I am seeing. I wish to say good-bye to them while I understand what I am doing."

"You're not making any sense, Hector."

Hector turned and looked once more at Jason. "I asked a few moments ago what was wrong with losing our minds. There is much wrong with it in the way that I am losing my mind. There are now long periods of time when I do not know who I am and I do not recognize anyone I know. Then I will awaken from these times and my mind is completely with me, as it is now. But these times do not last long. I do not know how long the other times last, or what I do or think during them. I just know that I awoke from such a time three days ago, and I was told about my son and his family. I decided that I must see them before I die, for I am sure that I will die soon."

"Oh my God," Jason said quietly, suddenly seeing Hector in a completely new light.

Hector smiled. "It is nothing to be sad about. I have led a very long life with which I am very satisfied. I will not die kicking and screaming and hoping to stay here because I am full of regrets. I wish to die at a time I choose and on my own terms. I do not want to be a vegetable in a bed who has no memory and who is not able to take what life has to offer me. But before I die, I wish to visit their graves."

"Wow." Jason was speechless. "I'm sorry," he finally said.

"It is not your fault. You do not need to apologize."

"Well no, that's not what I mean," Jason protested, but Hector turned to him and smiled again.

"I am only joking," he said. "I am ready to die. It is not a problem for me."

They sat for a few minutes, Jason's mind reeling from what he had learned. Finally, he got up. "I've got to go to the bathroom," he said. "You wanna get back on the road?"

"I am ready whenever you are," Hector replied. "Are you sure that you are ready? We have had a very long day so far, it seems."

"Yeah, we have. But I'm fine. If I get too tired, I'll just pull of the road and sleep again."

Hector nodded, and Jason walked off. He was torn between his admiration of Hector's way of getting him to think, of getting him to see things in ways he hadn't seen them before, and his new-found concern about Hector's condition. What did it mean when Hector said he didn't know who he was? What did he do? Would he be able to deal with it if Hector started being that way in the car?

He imagined that Hector had been quite a teacher in his day—probably the one that was always voted teacher of the year at whatever college he taught at. Jason wasn't used to learning lessons, especially from people he didn't even know. Too much of life seemed completely black and white to him, because that made life so much easier for him to understand. The further he got into shades of grey, the less clear things seemed; the less clear things seemed, the more frustrated and confused he became. And now Hector was telling him that he was creating this own idea of his own reality, and it actually made sense.

The bathroom was dark and it smelled bad, so he held his breath as much as he could and didn't spend a second more than he had to in there. It was hard for him to focus on anything at all, as Hector's words were still running through his mind. How much of what Jason was going through had he caused himself? How much of what he saw as other people hurting him was actually him hurting them? And when all was said and done, what did it matter who hurt whom? He was still on the highway to Seattle, and he still had a long way to go. All the people he had known were far behind him now.

And what must Hector be going through, not knowing how long he had until he lost his ability to think and to remember? How must he feel, just having found out that his son and his family had died?

Things were piling up quickly, and he had no real grasp on them at all.

He walked slowly back to the car, trying to enjoy using his leg muscles for as long as he could. He wasn't looking forward to getting back in the vehicle, but it was already late in the afternoon and the sun would be going down in a couple of hours—they might as well put some more miles behind them before dark. He looked out at the flow of cars streaming by in both directions on the highway, and he couldn't help but think of just how lucky they were to be underway still and not stuck back where the accident had happened with nothing but a damaged car.

"I wonder what happened to that girl's family," he said aloud as he came to his car, where Hector was leaning against the fender.

"I was thinking the same thing just now," Hector said. "It always is very tragic when people die, and I wonder what the plan is in the little girl's life if she has lost her parents."

"Personally, I'm not too sure there really is a plan. Maybe it's just the cruel hand of fate reaching down and screwing up her life from the very beginning."

"Life is not cruel, my friend. Life is a beautiful experience."

"Tell that to the little girl."

"The little girl must learn it for herself. That is something that one person cannot teach another person. Each of us must learn it in our own time, in our own ways, when we are ready for it. Not before."

"Whatever you say, amigo. I'm not sure I can agree with you on this one, though." Jason unlocked his door and reached in to push the button to unlock Hector's door, also.

"That is a surprise," Hector said with a trace of irony and humor in his voice. "I thought that young people always believed older people, out of respect for their elders."

Jason looked at him quickly and saw the glint in his eyes. He smiled. "Of course we do. We show nothing but respect for our elders, right?"

"That has not always been my experience. All in all, though, I am usually quite impressed by the amount of respect that most young people show." He got into the car, and Jason did the same. It was like stepping back into a particular world, one that he was inhabiting for now, one that enveloped him and held him in its grasp for as long as he was there. The car wasn't a place or an object for him any longer, but more like a state of being. In a way it was like a prison to him, a situation in which he had to put himself for long periods of time until he got to Seattle. He enjoyed the long road trips, but much of the romance of the memories had to do with the fact that memories of pains and stiffness and discomfort had faded.

Chapter Eight

The highway was crowded when they merged with the traffic, and Jason was quickly back in his driving mode, fully concentrated on the road and the other traffic that surrounded them. He wasn't in a talking mood, and he was somewhat thankful for the heavy traffic because it didn't allow him to think too much about other things. He didn't get the feeling that Hector was too interested in talking, either, as he was sitting quietly and looking out the window.

Soon he had to lower his visor to block the sun that was descending in the sky before him—avoiding the sunrise in the morning meant dealing with the sunset in the evening. Soon, he knew, the road would be reflecting the sun's light and it would be much more difficult to see clearly just how far ahead of him other cars were and just what they were doing. That was the time that he always liked to stop and eat, so he watched the distance signs to figure out where they would be able to stop for dinner for the hour or so that the sun would be at its worse. He couldn't believe that it was almost time for dinner already, as it seemed like just a few hours ago that they had stopped for breakfast. And what had happened to lunch? With all that had happened that day, they had simply forgotten to eat, it seemed. Surprisingly enough, he didn't feel hungry at all.

"Are you hungry?" he asked Hector about half an hour later. Neither of them had spoken since they had gotten back on the road, and even though he kind of liked the silence, Jason also found it kind of spooky. At least when Hector was talking, he didn't seem to be such a stranger. When he was just sitting there and not saying anything, though, Jason was reminded that up until just that morning, he had never seen Hector before in his life.

He had also never seen a dead person, and now he might have seen several—he had no way of knowing for sure, though. He couldn't shake the feeling that his world was different now, that he was different somehow. He felt like he had gone through some sort of hazing or transformational ceremony. Maybe what Hector had told him applied to him now—something inside of him had died, leaving him a much different person for the loss. But was he different in a better way, or in a worse way?

"I can eat whenever you want to eat," Hector told him. "As long as I eat, I am fine. It does not matter when."

"But don't you get hungry?"

"Of course I get hungry. But as I get older, the hunger does not bother me as it used to. Now it is just a feeling, neither pleasant nor unpleasant. It just is."

"Boy, I wish I could look at it that way. When I get hungry, I feel awful until I eat something."

"Hunger is simply your body's way of sending you a message. How you take that message is up to you."

"But don't you ever get weak and cranky when you're really hungry?"

Hector smiled. "I find that in this land where we have plenty of everything, I never truly get hungry, for I always know that I will be able to eat soon. Even if it is just a piece of bread, I will have something to eat. It does not help me to make more of my hunger than it truly is."

"What do you mean?"

"For many people in the world, hunger is a way of life. It kills many people every day, many children who have committed no crimes and who have done no wrong. Yet they die of starvation while we throw food away. When I remind myself that I am one of the people who throws food away, I remember that a small bit of hunger now and then is not a big thing."

"When you put it that way, it makes sense. It's just that to me, being hungry is one of the hardest things in the world. I don't know why. I guess I just never feel completely confident that I will end up eating. It's really weird. When I get hungry, I'm afraid I'm going to stay hungry."

"Did you go hungry as a child?"

"No, not really. Our parents fed us. We ate pretty well, actually. I remember that I used to be starving when I came home from school, though, but I wasn't allowed to eat anything until dinner. Mom and dad wouldn't let us fix our own food or grab a snack for the longest time because they were afraid we were going to mess up the kitchen or ruin our dinner by eating too much or something like that. So I'd come home starving, but I couldn't eat anything at all. My brother was much more practical—he'd always find something to eat, no matter what they said. Not me, though. I was the good one, the one who wouldn't disobey.

Sometimes by the time dinner came around I was too sick to eat, I was so hungry.

"I remember one time my mom brought home someone from work to have dinner. It might have been her boss—I don't know. But anyway, because we had a guest we were eating even later, so by the time dinner was ready my stomach hurt so bad that I was actually nauseous. I was almost crying, and I told my mom that I couldn't eat because I felt sick and I was afraid I would throw up. Then my dad got mad at me, and he called me a faker. He said that I didn't look sick, so I couldn't be that sick. That hurt me more than being hungry, I think, being called a liar like that. He sent me to my room and told me to go to bed if I was that sick, and then he didn't talk to me for like three days. I never did figure out why he got so mad, but it really hurt. He must have had a bad day at work or something.

"I just lay there in my bed, hating my dad and my stomach feeling awful. You know, I really had the feeling that for as little as he was actually at home, he didn't even have the right to discipline us or be mad at us. My brother felt the same way—we talked about it every once in a while, especially when we were being punished. It just wasn't fair that they could not be there for us all the time, but then expect us to do whatever they wanted us to do.

"I remember that night actually wishing he were dead, feeling that he had hurt me as deeply as was possible. I think that for that evening, I actually did hate him. I never felt much of a bond with him at all, but I usually didn't hate him.

"My brother came to my rescue that night—my little brother. It was going to turn out to be a pretty common thing, him coming to the rescue of his big brother in some way or another. He sneaked some food from the kitchen into my room, and he actually convinced me to eat it. I remember he started with a cookie, which was actually pretty easy to get me to eat. After I ate that, he gave me a slice of bread with peanut butter on it, folded over so it was like half a sandwich. I think he brought in a banana, too, but I'm not sure.

"After about half an hour, I felt fine. He and I started laughing and joking and playing, and then suddenly my dad opened the door. He didn't say anything. He just stood there, staring at me, and I knew as sure as he was looking at me that now he was sure that I had been faking it, now he was sure that I was a liar. I had been caught, somehow. I don't think he ever put two and two together—he never realized that I really was feeling sick because I was hungry, and of course I was going to start feeling better once I ate something.

"I think that moment was something that always stayed between us. I never again thought that he trusted me, no matter what I did, no matter how honest I was. And the worst part is that he was wrong—I wasn't lying, and I wasn't faking anything. It's pretty sad, but that was something that we never were able to grow past."

Hector stayed quiet for several minutes after Jason finished talking. "That is very sad," he finally said. "I would hate to know how many relationships are damaged because of misunderstandings such as this one."

"Probably more than three," Jason said. Hector looked at him with a question in his eyes. "Just a joke," Jason assured him. "Not a very good one, I guess."

"Not a very bad one, either," Hector said. "It just takes some thought to find the humor in it. The irony."

"Yeah, that's one of my curses—my sense of humor. Almost nobody gets my jokes. Some of them are pretty good, too, but they take too much thinking. It kind of sucks, because I'll never be someone who can liven up a party with a good joke or two."

"There are worse things in life than not having good jokes. You can buy a joke book. Memorize some of the jokes that others will find funny." He paused for a moment. "What is your brother's name?"

"I'm not sure, to tell you the truth. I always forget his name."

"That is another joke, no?"

"Yeah it is—the same one you told a while ago, I think. His name is Stephen."

"He sounds like a very nice young man. Do you see him much?"

"Sometimes. He moved over to Vermont after college, and I used to go over and see him on weekends. He just got engaged, actually, so I'm going to have to go back for his wedding in October."

"I am sure that he will be very glad to see you once more."

"Yeah, I guess so. He's pretty much into his job and his fiancée right now, and he's not completely thrilled with my, well, lifestyle, as he calls it. He thinks it's a choice I've made."

"That is a shame. The more we judge others and what they do, the more we hurt ourselves. But we always can justify it by saying that we know that we are right. I think many people will be surprised when they die and find out that there truly is no 'right' and no 'wrong' as we see them."

"I wish more people would see that before they die. It would sure make life much easier for the rest of us that have to put up with them and their judgment. Hey, there are some restaurants here—what do you say we stop and eat?"

"That will be fine," Hector said as Jason pulled onto the exit ramp. "You know, though, that 'putting up' with people is our choice. You do not have to put up with anybody if you do not wish to do so."

"Yeah, but I don't want to have to keep avoiding people just because I disagree with them or because they annoy me. Annoying them isn't exactly a positive thing either, is it?"

"Why do you think that you must avoid them? Why must it be either this or that? Why can you not simply let them be and accept them for who they are? If you simply accept them, they will annoy you much less."

"Accept them? When someone is judgmental and cruel and unfair, you think I should accept them?"

"Their actions and words are reflections of who they are and of where they are in their development. You want people to accept you for who you are, do you not?"

"Well, yeah, but—"

"But, but, but. We always have but's. If you wish others to accept you for who you are, then why should you not treat others the way you wish to be treated? Perhaps by accepting them for who they are, you may help them to grow into someone who is more positive and more caring. When you reject them or argue with them, you are telling them they are wrong, and that usually will cause them to hold on to their beliefs even more strongly than they would if they did not feel threatened."

Jason pulled into the parking lot of the lone non-fast-food restaurant and parked the car. "It sounds like you want me to be a saint, Hector. I'm not very good at that sort of thing."

"A saint?" Hector smiled. *"Dios mío, mijo.* There are no saints in this world. Except for mothers, of course. All people are equal—the people who are called saints have simply benefited from more extensive public relations. Did they not teach you of the Constitution at school?"

"I guess so, but probably in a class that I didn't pass. Civics was boring. Besides, what does the Constitution have to do with saints? We have separation of church and state, remember?"

"Not as much separation as we used to have, I think. But it is not the origin of the words that matters as much as their meaning. We all are created equal, and we all have the potential to be very great people. We just have many choices to make, and those choices help to determine the people we become."

Jason sighed and opened his door. "Oh, Hector—you make it sound so simple. I wish life were that simple."

"But it is, my friend. It is."

They entered the building to find a large room that could have been an inexpensive restaurant anywhere in the country—booths along the three walls, round tables in the middle, a small salad bar in among the tables, tasteful country-style wallpaper covering the walls and pleasant landscape lithographs hanging on them. Just inside the entryway was the end of a counter that held a cash register and a stack of menus. A cheerful girl about seventeen with blond hair pulled back into a ponytail and far too much make-up approached them and pulled a pair of menus from the stack. "Heather" was written on her name tag, and her green eyes were bright and clear. Jason was impressed with just how genuinely friendly she seemed. She was either the girl in school that everyone loved because she was so friendly or that everyone hated because she was so friendly—there didn't seem to be much middle ground in high school for people like her. Jason found himself hoping that she was the kind that was liked.

"Two?" she asked simply. "Smoking or non-smoking?"

"Non-smoking, please," Jason said, and she led them to a booth next to a window that offered a stunning view of the gas station next door.

They both thanked her as she set down the menus and left to get water, and then they picked up the menus and started to read. Within a few minutes they had ordered and started the wait for their food.

"Tell me about your wife," Jason said suddenly. He found himself suddenly somehow afraid that Hector might lose his ability to think and to tell stories, and he had no idea what he might do if that happened. Perhaps if Hector just continued to tell the stories, that might keep his brain on track. . . . "She sounds like a pretty wonderful woman."

Hector looked him in the eyes. "'Wonderful' does not even begin to describe her," he said, "but I thank you for the word. It certainly does apply to her. Leigh was a very bright light in a world that often seemed to do its best to put out the lights as much as it could. I think I can find a story that will tell you much more about her than I ever could describe her with my limited words. Words never are enough to describe a human being, you know. No matter what we say about someone, the picture we paint is always incomplete."

"Like that famous portrait of Washington?"

"Yes. And no. In that picture, we know exactly what is missing, no? Our minds can supply us with the details that our eyes cannot see. When you describe to me a person I never have met, I cannot know what is missing from your description. But when we hear a story about a person, then our minds can use what we hear to make a more complete picture of who the person is, not just what the person looks like or talks like or how she acts. And a story we can react to on our own terms, without the judgment of the story-teller insisting that we think a certain way. I think that we far too often are satisfied with descriptions and stories that are incomplete, and that need much more detail if they are to be accurate."

"Tell me a story about her, then."

"A story." Hector's eyes grew distant as he thought of his past, as he focused on something that existed only in his mind now, and Jason could see that he was suddenly very far away.

"You could see that Leigh was very special from the moment you noticed her for the first time. Many people disliked her because of that—it was impossible for some people not to feel threatened around her, for it was so obvious that she was special and that she knew it." Jason thought about their waitress, and his thoughts when he first saw her. "These other people, they were special, too, but they would not admit it to themselves or treat themselves as if they were. It is much easier to dislike a person who intimidates you through no fault of her own than it is to take the risk and get to know who she really is as a person.

"I must say that I was very lucky to meet her. Years later, I still could not believe that I had had the courage to approach her and talk to her as I did, for I was not a very courageous young man. I was too shy and too angry to be courageous.

"She was very confident, though many people saw her confidence as arrogance. They said that she was stuck up and that she was interested only in herself, yet I was fortunate enough to get to know her very well and learn that that was not the truth at all."

"I've known some people like that. Really nice people, but nobody would give them a break. It was like everyone was threatened by them. One of my college professors, especially."

"Yes, teachers often are seen that way. It is sad when they have much to teach, but people will not learn from them because they judge them too quickly. The children that Leigh taught, though, they loved her, and that was all that was important to her. She taught the third grade, which I believe is one of the most beautiful jobs of all. Children at that age are just very special, it seems—they are beginning to want to learn, but most of them have not yet learned the arts of judging others and trying to hurt others with their words. Some have, of course, but most have not.

"One day she invited me to her class to teach them something about Mexico. We had been married for four years then, and I had just finished my Master's degree in Spanish. The children were very well behaved and very polite. She and I had taken a trip to Guaymas the previous summer to visit the place where I was from, and we had many postcards and pictures to show the children."

Heather brought their food and a bottle of ketchup, and they both thanked her and told her no when she asked if they wanted anything else. With a bright smile she took her leave.

"Wow—that must have been interesting after all those years. Did you visit your family and all?"

Hector shook his head. "No—no, I did not. There was not much family left there. Only my grandmother, and she was very, very old. She had seen me only as an infant, and she did not recognize me as an adult. It was much like visiting a stranger."

"That's too bad."

Hector shrugged. "Perhaps. Perhaps not. It was perhaps better for me to realize that there was nothing there to pull me back to my native land. After that trip, I felt very little pull to leave Pocatello ever again, for there was nothing anywhere to pull me away. So I showed the class all of the pictures and I told them a little of the history of Mexico, and I even taught them a few words of Spanish. In those days, there were almost no languages ever taught in the grade schools. Americans were almost completely ignorant of other languages.

"Leigh sat in the back of the class. She did not speak much, because once she let someone else start talking, she did not like to interrupt. She did not feel threatened by the presence of someone else in the classroom, and she did not feel threatened that the children might like someone else more than they liked her. Some teachers fear that, you know."

"Boy, tell me about it. I had a teacher once in junior high who was so paranoid that we wouldn't like him that he never let anyone else in the classroom. One time someone from the office had to tell us something—something about a field trip we were going to take—and he took the paperwork from her and presented it himself. We were just in the seventh grade, but we sure recognized something weird when we saw it. And that guy was weird."

"My chicken is very good," Hector said. "And so are the potatoes. How is your food?"

"Good. Really good. But go on—I don't see a point to your story yet. I assume you're getting there?"

Hector smiled. "I am, indeed, getting there, *amigo*. The presentation was to me a joy, for there is nothing like seeing the eyes of children who are interested in listening to what you say. You can see their hearts and their spirits in their eyes, for most of them have not yet learned to hide those things, and they feel no desire to hide them in any case.

Even though the day outside was cold and dark and rainy, I felt very warm, very loved as only children can make one feel. So I gave all of my heart to it, and I got back much, much more than I gave—as one always does when one gives all that one has to give.

"When I finished, Leigh came to the front of the classroom. 'Let's thank Mr. Gutierrez for his wonderful presentation today. And do you know how we can give him a very special thank you?' She asked as if she did not want an answer. A rhetorical question. The children shook their heads and looked at her expectantly. 'How about if we give him a beautiful rainbow to take with him?' We all were very confused—I was just as confused as the children, for I had no idea what she was talking about. 'How can we give him a rainbow when it's still raining?' one of the little girls asked.

"Leigh just smiled. 'Perhaps it's not meant to come just right now,' she said. 'But it would make a great gift, wouldn't it?' Then she turned to me and said quietly 'I ordered one just for you.'

"She had done things like that before. It was like she could make things happen just because she wanted them to happen. She could turn a cloudy morning into a sunny afternoon, and she could stop an angry dog right in its tracks. She had a way about her—I believe that in another time they might have called her a witch, or a devil. I had gotten used to it, but I thought that she was just very good at seeing what would happen before it did. She was in tune with the world, and things did not come as surprises to her. She probably saw that the storm came from a certain direction and that there were breaks in the clouds that meant there soon would be a rainbow, but I do not know. 'Thank you very much,' I told her.

"And then I gathered up all of my stuff and thanked the children for their time and their patience and their attention, and I started to leave the room. Just then, one of the little boys by the window said 'Look at the rainbow!' There was a note of awe in his voice. And we all looked out the window to see the most beautiful, the brightest double rainbow that I ever had seen. The sun had shone through somewhere behind the school, and there in front of the school the rainbow filled the sky right in front of a bank of very dark clouds.

"But even better than the rainbow was seeing the look on the children's faces. They were captivated. Most of them had their mouths wide open in awe, and some of them managed to say 'Wow!' Leigh just looked at me with a smile. The most amazing thing to me, though, was that I was not in the least bit surprised. To me it somehow seemed natural, something that was spectacular but certainly not out of the ordinary. I smiled back at her. I turned to the children and bowed. 'Thank you very much,' I said to them. 'Your gift is very beautiful, and I will carry it with me always.' Then I left."

"Wow," Jason said. "I think that would really freak me out."

Hector shook his head. "Not if you had known Leigh," he said quietly. "This was a woman whose smile could enchant even the most cynical of people, someone who always knew just the right words for every situation, whether she was with adults or with children. She truly was a magnificent person, and if there was something that was not normal, then it almost was expected. I came to expect the unexpected when I was with her. And since. I carry that rainbow with me even until today."

"Do you have any other stories like that one? About her, I mean."

Hector looked at Jason and held his gaze there, as if challenging him somehow, but he didn't say anything for several very long moments. Jason avoided looking into Hector's eyes until he couldn't avoid it any longer, then met his gaze.

"What?" Jason asked.

Hector sighed, then looked at Heather, who was bringing them their dessert. "Do you know what it means to kibitz?" he asked Jason.

Jason thanked Heather for his ice cream. "I've heard the word," he said to Hector. "Isn't it some sort of game with dice or something?"

"No, it is not a game. One who kibitzes is a person who always watches games—like chess—and gives suggestions to the players. They are not playing themselves, but they are trying to be part of the game."

Jason looked at him curiously. "And. . . .?" he asked.

"Miguel de Unamuno once wrote a story about just such a man. This man always would come to the place where other people were playing chess, and he would watch them, always watch them. As time went on, the men who were playing chess became infuriated with him, and he could not understand why. They finally explained to him that they did not appreciate the fact that they were making the effort to play, they were thinking and making moves and defending their pieces and putting their hearts into their games, but this man, he was contributing nothing to the games, nothing to the lives or the knowledge of the other men. He was taking, taking, taking, but giving nothing back. He was contributing no challenges, he was helping no one to better themselves."

"Yeah, but so what? What's wrong with watching these guys if they were playing anyways?"

"That is exactly what he thought. So what? You are playing here, so why should I not watch? But to the men playing the game, he was taking from them—he was using them to make his life richer, but that was all. It was like free entertainment to him, and he gave nothing back for it. He was learning much, every day, from the effort and the skill of these other men, yet he was contributing nothing to their lives. If he played once in a while, they would have had no problem, even if he were to lose badly every time. But he would not play."

"So are you saying that I should contribute some stories here?"

Hector smiled. "I am saying no such thing. Anything like that would be completely your own decision. I am simply telling you of a story that I just remembered."

"I guess I am kind of being like that guy, listening to all the stories about you and your life, but not telling you anything about mine."

"You have told me something of your life."

"Yeah, I guess I have. Then why tell me about the story about the guy who wouldn't play chess?"

"I have told you. I simply told you the plot of a story that I remembered. Perhaps there is relevance to it, perhaps there is none. The important thing is what you take from it, not what I have meant by it."

"You're too funny, Hector," Jason sighed. "And from what I've learned about you so far today, there's got to be relevance to the story. But what do you say we get out of here? It's already dark, and we still have miles to go before we sleep."

"Miles to go before we sleep," Hector said with a smile.

The evening was still warm, and once again they were treated to the incessant sounds of wheels flying over the pavement of the highway and the engines that propelled the vehicles forward. Jason looked out at the highway.

"It never stops, does it?" he asked, standing next to his car.

"Never," Hector said. "To me, it is very sad. I would like to make a law that for one day, nobody may go anywhere. People must stay at home with their families, or if they have no families they must be with friends, or they must do something that is relaxing and enjoyable near their own homes so they could walk there. The automobile is a beautiful invention, but it is another one that we have allowed to take over our lives. We no longer have cars to serve us, for we let them rule our lives and we serve them. We keep them clean, we feed them, we pay to have them maintained. We decorate them and we pay much money to fill them with things that are unnecessary, such as expensive stereos and even video players. And at this moment all over the world there are highways filled just as this one is. At this very moment, millions of people are inside of their metal boxes, flying towards their destinations, going somewhere."

"You make that sound like a bad thing."

"Bad?" Hector shook his head. "No, I do not believe it is bad. As I have said before, it simply is as it is. But it is sad that so many people spend so much time going back and forth between jobs and tasks and things to do, while so few people are able to slow down and spend time quietly with themselves. Most of the people I know never are relaxed because they know that sometime soon they must be somewhere else, and they do not want to be late to something 'important.' I know people who almost never see their own children, their own wives."

"Like my parents. I guess you're right—it is kind of sad, isn't it? I wonder how many of those people out there on the highway absolutely have to be there. That trucker does—" he pointed to an 18-wheeler barreling by—"because that's his job. I don't know about the guy in the car behind him, though."

"That is just the problem," Hector said. "We do not
know. There is so much in this world that we do not know
that what we do know is perhaps as one grain of sand on a
very large beach. When we look at all these cars we do not
know what is going on in the lives of the people inside of
them. Perhaps every single person in every single car must
be there at this moment. Perhaps half of them could find
jobs closer to their homes that paid less money but gave
them more free time. Perhaps one-third of them choose to
be on the road because as long as they are closed up in their
cars, they do not have to deal with other human beings, and
they enjoy the sense of solitude and the sense of power and
independence that they have when they are all alone in their
vehicles. There is much fear in the world, you know."

"Oh, yeah—I'm well aware of that. I've got plenty of it
myself."

"As do all of us."

"You, too, Hector? What are you afraid of? It seems to
me that you're not afraid of anything. If you were to ask
me, I'd say you had things pretty much under control."

Hector laughed. "Don't you think it is time for us to get
on the road?"

"That's avoidance, Hector." They both got into the car.
"I didn't peg you as the avoiding type," Jason said as he
closed his door.

"It is very difficult to avoid anything when we are in such
a very small space, no?"

"Difficult, but not impossible. Tell me, what do you have
to be afraid of?"

"For one thing, I am afraid that I might not make it to
Pocatello to see my son's grave before I lose my mind once
more and am unable to know where I am."

Jason was surprised at the words, and he looked at
Hector. "We'll make, it, Hector."

Hector smiled.

Chapter Nine

"What do you say," Jason asked as he backed out of the parking space and started out once more, "shall we join the dance of the lonely and isolated once more?"

"It is a dance that never does end. It only slows down as it did this morning, then it speeds back up again."

"And it keeps pulling people into itself, doesn't it? I bet a lot of people in it don't even realize where they are or what they're doing or where they're going."

"How many of those people do you think actually care about where they are or where they are going?"

Jason thought it over. "Probably most of them, I would guess."

"Most of them? Do you not think that if you cared about where you are, you would realize where you are?"

Jason laughed. "Okay, you got me there. You're right—I contradict myself. But I'd have to say that I think that most people would say that they cared. Or they would say that they were aware."

"You probably are right. But most people care only that their illusions are fulfilled. They spend their time and energy trying to make happen what they think should happen. They never trust life to be what life should be."

At that moment a large gooey something smashed into the windshield right in the middle of Jason's view. It was much larger and much more disgusting than the remains of the many other insects that had died on his windshield.

"Oh, great," Jason said. "Why do they always do that? Right smack in front of me, too. That's gonna make driving fun."

"I will clean it off if you will stop the car," Hector said. "It looks like it was a moth. It probably was attracted by the many headlights on the highway." He reached into his pocket and pulled out some napkins. "It will take me only a second."

Jason turned on his blinker and edged into the breakdown lane, slowing down quickly to a stop. He turned on his emergency flashers.

"I can get it, Hector," he said.

"It is not a problem." Hector's door was open in a flash, and he was out of the car before Jason knew what was happening. He watched as Hector moved to the front of the car and waited until the traffic allowed him to approach the windshield on the driver's side. In just a moment he had cleaned the mess and was back in the car.

"Thanks, Hector," Jason said. "I could have done it, though. You didn't have to."

"Of course I did not have to. But I wanted to."

Jason put the car into first and checked his mirrors, surprised to find that there was no one behind him for quite a distance. He pulled into the right lane and sped up quickly, soon reaching the speed limit and a bit beyond.

"I feel kind of sorry for those bugs," Jason said. "They never know what hit them, do they?"

"Probably not. But would that not be the best way to go? Or at least among the best ways to go?"

"I don't know. Possibly. I think the best way to go would be peacefully, to die in your sleep. I've never been one of those people who think it's better to go in a blaze of glory and all that crap. I kind of like the idea of fading away, you know?"

"It certainly does have its appeal, does it not? It sounds like a peaceful way to pass from this world to the next."

"If there is a next world. I'm not sure that I believe in a next world."

"But your belief does not make it exist or not exist, does it?"

"What do you mean?"

"If there is a God, but someone does not believe in him, does God cease to exist?"

Jason thought for a moment. "Maybe he does. Maybe it's our belief in God that makes him exist in the first place."

Hector looked at him with a pleased look on his face. "That is the second thing I have heard from you that shows that you think past the surface, *mi amigo*. Thank you for sharing that thought with me."

"You're welcome," Jason said dryly. "You don't have to be so happy about it."

"But of course I do. You have shown something that is very important for young people to show, and that is that you are willing to challenge the beliefs and the views of reality that you have been taught your entire life. There are very few people in the world who teach that our belief in God creates God. For most people, those words would be blasphemy. But one does not even have to believe in such a statement to make it—no, the most important thing is to entertain the notion, if even for just one moment. That is what can ultimately free us from the beliefs that we have been given by our fathers and mothers and aunts and uncles."

"Wow, you really are happy about it." Jason was amazed at Hector's sudden animation. "Well, I'm glad that I was able to make you happy."

"As am I, my friend—as am I. But tell me, Jason—you did not finish your story earlier. Why have you left your home? Why are you leaving behind the people who have been a part of your life for so long?"

"Why shouldn't I?"

"I do not say that you should not do so. No, perhaps the very best thing for you at this point in your life is to leave behind the people who have been a part of your life and start completely anew. Perhaps you never would be able to continue your journey, your growth, if you were to stay where you were with the people you were with. I simply ask, why?"

Jason sighed deeply, staring straight ahead at the road and the white line that stretched never-ending on the right side of the road. "It's a pretty long story, Hector. I've already told you most of it."

Hector shrugged. "I have nothing better to do right now than listen to the rest of a long story."

"But I'm not sure that I want to tell it."

"That is okay," Hector replied. "I am not sure that I want to hear it. But I am willing to take the risk and hear it anyway."

Jason laughed. "That's right sporting of you, chap," he said in his best English accent.

Hector looked at him in surprise. "Have you been to Australia?"

"Australia? That was supposed to be an English accent. Couldn't you tell?"

Hector sighed. "No, I could not. To be honest, they all sound alike to me."

"Hey, speaking of accents, maybe you could tell me why you still have such a strong one if you've lived in the states pretty much all your life. Why is it that you still have such a strong Mexican accent?"

"That is easy, my friend," Hector said with a smile. "I still have an accent because I wish to have an accent. It reminds me of my heritage, and it reminds me of my mother and father without keeping me stuck in my past. It is a very important part of me. But if you want me to," he continued, now speaking with no trace of an accent at all, "I can speak American for you and you'll never have any idea where I'm from."

Jason looked over at him in surprise. "You've gotta be kidding me. You can do that whenever you want? Switch like that?"

"If I wish. Just as I can switch from English to Spanish. I sometimes spoke like that when I taught at the college, especially in the earlier years. Recently, there is much talk of cultural diversity and diversity studies, so an accent such as mine often is a positive thing. You see, students often learn more from you if they believe that you are something other than you truly are. Years ago, though, when there was much more prejudice against Mexicans, I often would speak with my American accent."

"What a shame that people could have something against you just because of where you're from."

"Perhaps it is a shame. Perhaps it has been a blessing for me; perhaps I have learned much about myself because of other people's prejudices that I never would have learned otherwise. We never can know."

Jason sighed again. "You know, it's really annoying that you can always see two sides to everything. Wouldn't you like sometimes to just get pissed off and enjoy being pissed off?"

"You must be careful, Jason. Being angry is always negative energy. There are times when anger is perhaps appropriate, but when we stay angry for the sake of being angry, we spread much negative energy in the world. I believe that there is enough negative energy in the world without me contributing to it, also. Anger is a destructive emotion, not a constructive one."

"You've got an answer for everything, don't you?"

"Of course I do! I am an old man, and I have been on this planet many years. I hope that I should have some answers. I would not say that they always are the right answers—just the answers I have learned."

"That's something, though. At least you have some answers. I usually feel like everything in my life is a question, like there are no answers for anything that happens to me."

"But that is normal at your age, no? You are still building and learning, no?"

"And tearing down and destroying. And running away."

"From what are you running, my friend?"

Jason turned and looked at Hector in the darkness for a few moments, so long that Hector started to worry that he might drive the car off the road. Then he smiled and looked forward once more. There was no humor in the smile, though.

"My partner and I were together for three years, you know. It was a really nice life. We had a great apartment, really nice friends, always someplace to go and something to do. We were either inviting people over to our place, or people were inviting us over to theirs. Believe it or not, we didn't find much prejudice at all because we were gay—people treated us very well. There were a few jerks and a few rude comments every now and then, but I guess you can never get away from that. I loved my job, too—I was working in the personnel department at an insurance company. People were really nice to me there, and I was good at what I did. I got like three raises my first two years there. It was a perfect place for me.

"Lance—that was my partner's name—worked as a manager at one of those electronics superstores. His hours were really weird, and he didn't like his job much. They had a really hard time finding people to work for them who were reliable, so he had to work a lot when people wouldn't show up for work or something like that. But when we spent time together, it was always great. We used to go for long drives on weekends, just to get away and get out of town. We went skiing in the winter a lot. We'd try to find nice little restaurants or cafes in nice little towns, places where we could sit down and relax and not feel any pretension or stress at all. So many of the places in town were full of people who had so many expectations of others. It was really annoying, and it was great to get away from it.

"He and I met four years ago, and we started seeing each other exclusively three years ago. He's a great guy, in most ways. Very kind and considerate, very caring, very reliable. He was a good cook, too, so that was kind of a bonus for me. We always had microwaved dinners when I was growing up, so to have the chance to eat some real cooking that was really good was something new.

"I always wondered what he was doing with me—I always asked myself what he could see in me when there were so many others he could have been with. What was so special about me? I still don't see that, and I'm not sure that I ever will. Claudia, a friend of mine, tells me that I need to see it or else I'm going to keep pushing people away from me, but I'm not sure what she means by that. Or at least, I wasn't sure until I started talking to you."

He stared straight ahead silently for almost two minutes without saying a word. Hector stayed quiet, waiting and listening.

"I think now I do know what she meant, though. Maybe in part I drove Lance away from me. Maybe I drive other people away. I do lose friends, people that I just kind of lose touch with over the years. Maybe it was me who drove Lance to start seeing someone else about a year ago. I just found out about it a few weeks ago and I wanted to blame it all on him, but I guess I have to take some of the responsibility for the situation, don't I?"

"I am not sure that any of us ever can take responsibility for the actions of any other persons," Hector said quietly. "People make their own decisions. We may influence them, but do we cause them? Perhaps they blame those decisions on us, but in the end they are still a person's own decisions to make, no?"

"I don't know. Maybe. I just kind of wish that Lance had told me that he was seeing someone else, because I sure would have liked to know. But he never did tell me. I had to find out myself when a friend told me. She couldn't keep it from me any more, she said, because she didn't like knowing that I was being cheated on without me knowing about it. If she hadn't had a bit of sympathy for me, I still might not know what he was doing."

"That is very sad," Hector said. "I am sorry that you had to go through it. No one deserves to be treated that way."

"Yeah, well, that's not the half of it," Jason replied. "Once I found out what was going on, I confronted Lance and he decided that he was going to move out immediately and move in with the guy he was seeing. He left the apartment and left me alone to figure out what I was going to do. He said he was sorry, but he didn't say it as an apology. I didn't want to hear it, so it didn't matter how he said it. I had a very hard time trusting people to begin with, and probably the worst thing in the world for me was to have someone violate my trust so badly. Anyway, I was doing my best to hang in there and fight the depression that kept trying to come around. I was all set to move into another apartment to get away from all the memories when Lance called. I thought he was just trying to patch things up or that he had left something at the apartment. I wish that's what it was.

"I didn't have any such luck, though. He told me that the guy he had moved in with—the guy he had been seeing behind my back for a while—had just been tested, and it turns out that he's HIV-positive. HIV—the real thing. And all of a sudden my life is turned even more upside-down than it was before, because now I don't have any idea if I'm carrying the virus or not. It's too early to tell. Even Lance doesn't know if he has it. All of a sudden my entire life is completely different. I can't plan on a future any more, because I don't even know if I have a fucking future. I might be dead in two years, and I might live to be a hundred damn years old. There may be something inside me right now that's starting the slow process of killing me in a few years, just working at its own leisure, slowly tearing down my body."

He stopped, unable to talk any more. Hector noticed that his hands gripped the steering wheel tightly, and Jason was fighting to hold back his tears.

They drove on in silence for a long while. There was no sound in the car except that of the engine humming and the wheels speeding over the pavement. Jason fought the urge to turn on the radio—he wasn't enjoying the silence, but he didn't feel like listening to any music at the moment.

Hector sat quietly, his fingertips pressed together before him as if he were meditating. Jason would have liked to know what he was thinking, but in his silence there was no indication of what that might be. He stared straight ahead into the pool of light that the headlights made on the highway, and into the darkness beyond that, at the taillights of the cars that were far ahead of them.

"What will you do?" Hector asked finally, after a good ten minutes had passed.

Jason thought for a moment. "What do you mean?"

"With your life. What will you do with your life now?"

"Well, I'm not dead yet. I don't even know if I'll end up getting AIDS. I guess I'll just keep getting tested over and over and over until something comes up positive. Or not. If it doesn't, though, I'll never know how much I can trust a negative result. What if it's a false negative? I guess I'll just have to become a monk now and live in isolation. I certainly don't want to risk anyone else's health, you know."

"That is very noble of you," Hector said.

"I guess," Jason said. "I just couldn't live with myself if I thought of me putting someone else at any risk at all. It's just not worth it."

"You face some very difficult times ahead now. Your future is full of the unknown and the unknowable in many ways."

"Just like that little girl," Jason muttered.

"What?" Hector asked.

"Just like the little girl this morning," Jason explained. "I would hate to think of what her future will be like, especially if her parents were dead. She's going to have a pretty hard life ahead of her."

"Yes, she will," Hector agreed. "But she will make it. As will you."

"Probably. It's different, though. She has her whole life ahead of her. I don't know how much I have ahead of me."

"And I do not know how much I have ahead of me, either. But that is not what is important."

"Oh, yeah? Then what is important? What we do with the time we have left?"

"What is important is what we do with each moment as we live it. We cannot focus on the time we have left, for none of us knows how much there is. If we make a five-year plan and we live for only two, then much of what we planned never will come to be. The important thing is to live each moment, every moment that we have as human beings, as well as we can."

"Like this moment right now? What's so special about right now? How can we make this special when all we're doing is sitting in a car heading west on a highway?"

Hector smiled. "I suppose the important question is what you consider to be special. Most people think that special moments are the extraordinary ones, the ones that we will remember all our lives, such as the moment you meet the person you love or the time that you throw the pass that wins the football game. In life, though, every moment is special. Right now we are having an interesting conversation, and I am learning much about life from you. I believe that in our current situation, an interesting conversation is one of the best possible ways to spend our moments. We also could spend them resting, or listening to music, or listening to a program on a tape. The important thing is that we give the moment all of the attention that we have, for it deserves all the attention that we can give to it. And if we give it all of our attention, it will give back to us all of its secrets."

"Secrets?" Jason laughed; it wasn't a mocking or a derisive laugh, but a bemused one that reflected his confusion. "What kind of secret is this moment giving to you, Hector? I can't see any secrets."

"That is only because you do not yet know what to look for, my friend. Each moment that we live is full of secrets, and as we learn to see what those secrets are, they become our secrets, too. They one day will become just as important a part of your life as anything else is. Leigh taught me how to look for the importance that each moment carries in it, and I only wish that I had learned it from her earlier, so that we could have shared the knowledge in our lives."

"What do you mean? What happened to her?"

"Why, she died, of course," Hector said, not a trace of sadness in his voice. "Hers was the most beautiful death that I ever have seen. I hope that when I die, I can die as beautifully as she."

"Beautiful? How can a death be beautiful?"

Hector sighed. "Anything can be beautiful, Jason. Even the horrible, the awful. Many people say this is how evil can be so seductive—it has a beauty that is beyond description, and those who see it and recognize the beauty are pulled into its trap, for they feel that anything that is beautiful must be good. But not all that is beautiful is good, though I can assure you that all that is good is beautiful."

"I'll have to take your word on that. I'm not quite sure that I buy it, but since you've been around longer than I have, I'll have to trust you."

"Thank you. I am flattered."

Jason laughed. "I guess you should be now, shouldn't you?" He paused a few moments. "How did Leigh die?" he asked. "How was it beautiful?"

Hector sat quietly for a few very long moments.

"I'm sorry," Jason finally said, afraid that Hector's silence meant that he didn't want to answer the question. "I guess it's really none of my business."

"No, no, no," Hector said reassuringly. "I am not quiet because I do not want to answer. I am quiet because I do not want to answer without thinking first, without knowing that the words that I say do justice to Leigh. I do not want to say anything that will lessen the experiences that I have had with her."

"She was that special."

"I never will know just how special she was. Most of us never realize the depth of other people's hearts and souls. We are allowed to see only the surface, and every once in a while, someone offers us a glimpse into their depths, a short, quick glance into who they truly are and what they truly consist of as human beings. It was like that with Leigh for me. I saw only a glimpse of what she truly was, and that glimpse was enough to teach me more than I have learned from anybody else in my life."

"I knew someone like that once. In college. She was a very good friend. So I can imagine what it must have been like with someone you were in love with."

"One day I came home from school near the end of the spring semester. It was a beautiful day in May, the kind that the birds wait for to sing their best, the kind that opens up your heart that has been waiting through the spring rains and the still-cold days of April that frustrate the part of you that waits so impatiently for summer. The trees were still the bright green of spring, just before they took on the darker hues for the summer. The air was light and clear and fresh, and the breeze touched your skin just lightly enough to cool you.

"Leigh usually came home later than I, but on that day she was there at home, sitting in her favorite chair. She had moved it from the living room into the dining room, in front of the large picture window that looked out into our back yard. I believe she was watching the birds eat at our feeder and the squirrels play in the trees and on the lawn. The late-afternoon sunshine poured through the window and lit everything in that soft glow that you get only during the twilight hours. Everything seemed to be tinged with gold, a glowing gold that made the scene so peaceful that I wanted to cry. At that moment I wished that I had become a painter, for never before had I looked at a scene that was so perfect in all ways.

"Leigh sat motionless in her chair. She was staring straight ahead, and her face was as peaceful as I ever had seen it. She didn't even look up when I came in. Neither of us said hello—we had long ago stopped needing to hear the other one greet us. We knew that the greeting was there, and that was enough.

"I pulled up a chair from the table and put it next to her chair. We were in our very early fifties then, and Leigh's face had grown even more into a face of peace, of love, of support. When you looked at her, you knew that you were looking into the face of someone who would help you in any way that she could, who would love you unconditionally. Unless you were one who hurt others—then you knew you were looking into the eyes of someone who would not allow you to get away with anything that was bad or evil. She had crow's feet at the corners of her eyes, for she had smiled so much in her life. That day, though, something was different, though I could not figure it out. The smile in her eyes was not the usual smile. It was still there, but its message that day was not its usual message.

"As I looked over at her face there in the afternoon's soft and gentle light, I saw that there were tears in her eyes. They probably were not tears of sadness, I suspected, but they were there nonetheless. I did not ask her why, for I trusted that she would tell me when it was right for her to tell me. And she would be ready to tell me when she felt that I was ready to hear.

"When she finally spoke, she did not move her eyes at all. She still stared straight ahead, focused on the birds on the feeder.

"'The doctor called today,' she told me. I was surprised, because she hadn't told me anything out of the ordinary about her examination the week before when I had asked her about it. She had told me that it was just another exam in that tone of voice that said 'Let's drop this,' so I had dropped it.

"I did not answer. I did not need to. I knew that she knew what I was thinking, and I knew that she would tell me more as she could.

"'The cancer is back,' she said simply, and all of a sudden, in one extremely short moment, I felt my world fall apart. I felt the greatest fear that I ever had felt in my life, and it was the fear of a life without Leigh. I suppose that one could say that I had become addicted to her, but I prefer to think that I was simply so deeply in love with her that I could not imagine what my life would be like without the object of my strongest love.

"Years before, she had had ovarian cancer, and she had to have a hysterectomy. Of course, we hoped that the doctors had gotten it all, but we all know that there is no way to be sure of that if you are a doctor. It also is impossible to guarantee that the cancer will not come back.

"'When will you start the chemotherapy?' I asked her, but somehow even as I was asking the question, I knew what her answer would be. She turned to me and smiled a melancholy but strong smile. 'I won't,' she said.

"She and I had talked about this possibility years before, when she first had the cancer, and she said many times that she did not want to go through the chemotherapy and the surgeries a second time. They took too much out of her, she said, and she did not want to live her life dreading the day ahead every day that she woke up. She had no fear of death at all—she saw it as a great adventure, passing on to another reality. She believed in God, but not in a religious way. She had a true relationship with God, I believe, and I truly envied her that. I still do. She was at peace with the whole world, it seemed, and nothing could rattle her for more than a few minutes.

"I sat there with her for a very long time, holding her hand. Neither of us spoke. There were no words that could express what we wanted to say. In my heart I wanted to try to talk her into the chemotherapy, into trying to extend her life every possible moment, but I knew that was my own selfishness trying to guide me, that I was not trying to ask for what was best for Leigh. Besides, I had promised her before that I would not do so. She had the right to make the decisions that were best for her.

"Of course, knowing that did not make it any easier for me."

"That must have been pretty hard."

"It could have been, but in the end it was easier than you might think. I did not want to lose Leigh's company, and I did not want to say good-bye to her forever, but what is forever? I do not believe that our lives end when our bodies stop working, so it would be silly of me to think that Leigh is actually dead. I believe that she lives on, as do all the other people who have lived in this beautiful world of ours. One day we will go to join them, unless they already have moved on to somewhere else by the time we get there."

Hector laughed. "I do not know what to call it. Leigh and I used to talk about heaven a lot. She objected to the idea of there being streets paved with gold and jewels in the walls. She said that was more an indication of what ignorant people considered to be important here on earth than it was of what God might make the perfect place for us like. How many people have been murdered, enslaved, destroyed for gold and jewels? Why would we want them in heaven? Most of our ideas about heaven are pretty silly."

"I guess you could say that."

"Hell is the same way. If you promise people awful eternal punishments if they do not do something the 'right' way, it is easier to keep them from doing what you wish them not to do. If you promise them rewards for doing things that 'right' way, it is easier to get them to do what you wish them to do. Leigh used to say that heaven is as a cookie to a child, while hell is the same as a spanking. It is not the actual cookie that gets a child to act right, but the promise of a cookie. And it is the threat of a spanking that can keep children from doing certain things. Heaven and hell make us all little children."

"That makes sense. I've always had problems with the idea of heaven and hell, but I could never put it into words."

And when you add to those ideas the ridiculousness of a God of supposed unconditional love who is ready to punish people for eternity just because they have made mistakes, then the idea of heaven and hell grows even more silly. Leigh believed that she was moving on to be with God, but she didn't feel a need to define or describe what that was going to be like. I admire her for that. That is what helped her to die beautifully—she was willing to accept what came without trying to control everything about it. Her one effort at control was to take medicine for the pain."

"So how did she die beautifully, then? What does that mean?"

"I suppose that it would mean something different to each person. To me it meant that she died without complaint, without ever saying a word such as it was not fair that she had to get cancer, without ever blaming her doctors for what they could not do for her. It meant that she left this world with encouragement for the rest of us, and that she provided us with some very special moments before she left, moments in which she never once talked about what she was going through, but when she talked about the many things that we had gone through together and how special they were to her.

"I will remember always the last day that I spent with her. We were at home, because she did not want to die in a hospital. She had grown very weak, and she slept much of the time. It was a Saturday afternoon in the late summer, very soon after she had learned of the new cancer. The sun was shining very brightly. I had moved her bed very close to the window of our bedroom so that she always could see the trees, which were her favorite things. When Leigh awoke that day, I was sitting in my armchair next to the bed. I sat there and read very often, just to be near her. Even though she would not have wanted to impose upon me, I still felt that she needed me. I don't know—perhaps I simply felt a need to be needed by her.

"She smiled at me when she awoke. Then she looked outside at the brilliant blue sky and her eyes grew wide in wonder, just as a child's would have. 'I'll miss the trees,' she said quietly.

"I put down my book and leaned closer to her. I did not know what to say. I wanted to say, 'And I will miss you,' but it not seem appropriate. Finally, I said, 'I still have the rainbow that you and the children gave me,' and she turned to look in my eyes. It made me feel very good to see the love and the wonder there, to see that she still was able to appreciate the beauty of the world. I always have felt that the trees in our yard were God's last gift to her while she was on this planet, for right then she breathed her last breath. It was a very deep breath, and when she breathed out, I felt her accepting whatever was coming. She closed her eyes, and then she breathed no more."

Jason was silent. He glanced over at Hector, who seemed to be staring off into space once more, lost in thought. "What did you do?" he asked.

Hector smiled sadly. "My friend, there was nothing for me to do. I sat with her for a while, and I thought of all our life together from the very first time that I saw her, and I felt a great sense of joy. I thought of what life would be like without her, and I felt a great sense of loss. I thought of all that she had given to others while she was alive and that she would be able to give no more, and I felt a sense of sadness. I thought of how much I had changed as a person because of all that she had taught me about life, and I felt very, very grateful. I knew that God had created a very special woman in Leigh, and I still could not believe that I had had the honor of having her as a wonderful and important part of my life."

"I wouldn't mind having someone like that in my life," Jason said quietly. "It would be nice to feel that way about someone. Maybe even to have someone feel that way about me."

Hector shrugged. "Perhaps there already is someone like that in your life. Perhaps you will meet that person three months from next Tuesday. Or in five years. Or twelve. We never know what will happen to us each day that we live. It is for us to keep ourselves open to possibility and potential. Too many people look at life as impossibilities and obstacles."

"Yeah, well it can get kind of hard to see everything as possible when there are so many people telling you all that things that you can't do or shouldn't do, or criticizing the things you try to do so that you don't even want to try to do them again."

"It is not nearly as hard as you think, *mijo*. You just have to decide who you allow to affect the way that you see the world. Leigh saw the world as she wished to see the world. Nobody's actions or words changed the way she saw it. She made the decisions to make her responses to other people be positive in her life."

"And I admire her for that, really, I do. When I was a kid, though, it was really hard to see the world that way when my parents kept telling me what I should do and how I should see the world."

"Yes, it is much harder when we are young. But you are a child no longer—why do you choose to continue to carry around lessons that no longer serve you, that continue to hurt you? If they do not help you in your life, why do you still keep them with you?"

"I guess because I'm just not enlightened enough yet to let go of them. I don't know—I feel like they're a part of me. My dad always seemed to think that the world was against him somehow, that life was always some kind of battle. We always learned that we had to look after ourselves, to take care of ourselves, to look out for number one, you know? Everything was competition. I think that's why I was such a disappointment to my father—I wasn't very good at competing. I wasn't a good baseball player, or football player, or basketball player. I just didn't like to compete. And there's never been a Leigh in my life to tell me that's okay."

"But there will be," Hector said kindly. "Please be patient, Jason. You will find the right person for you, someone who knows that life is meant to be about cooperation, not competition. Someone who knows that we are not here to battle one another, but to assist each other."

Jason laughed. "You need to sit down and have a heart-to-heart with my dad, then. He certainly could learn a thing or two from you. I remember when he signed me up for Little League. I was on the Astros, and you can imagine the nickname that the other kids gave our team. I wasn't very good, and it wasn't a whole lot of fun to play. But they had this rule that every kid on the team had to play in every game, so I was in there every game. One game they put me out in right field, which is where they usually put me so I could do as little damage as possible, and someone hit a fly ball to me. I don't know why, but I just froze up—completely froze. I started to try to run towards the ball, because I knew that I could catch it, but my legs wouldn't work. I watched that ball fly towards me in slow motion, and I kept trying to move but I couldn't. It landed between me and the center fielder, and he had to field it.

"My dad pretty much hit the roof. It was like the only game of mine that he had ever gone to, and that had to happen then. He wouldn't even talk to me in the car, except for one thing that I'll never forget. He said he wouldn't have minded if I had missed the ball, as long as I tried for it. But I wasn't even willing to try, he said, and he had never felt so ashamed in his life. Of me."

"That must have been very painful," Hector said quietly.

"You could say that. It was actually pretty devastating. We already had a poor relationship, and I was only seven years old, trying to play a game that I didn't even want to play just to please my dad. And now he was ashamed of me. I didn't want to freeze up, and I don't know why I did. But I knew from that moment that I would never be able to please my father. I think he knew that then, too. So I just kind of gave up on the idea of my father ever being proud of me."

"And gave up on the idea of anyone else being proud of you, ever."

"Maybe," Jason admitting quietly.

Hector sighed.

"But what does this mean, Hector?" Jason asked, perplexed. "I mean, it's one thing to know what happened and to see how something affected you when you were a kid, but it's another thing entirely to put it behind you and live your life without having it affect you all the time."

"This is very true."

"So what do I do about it?"

"What do you think you do about it?"

Jason turned to look at Hector, pretending to be upset at having his question thrown back at him. In the glow of the instrument panel, he suddenly saw Hector's age in his face and his posture. Hector looked older than he had before, more tired, more worn down. Jason thought about all the years that Hector had lived, all of the things he must have seen in his life, all of the people he must have known. For just a moment, he had an image of himself at that age, and he wondered what kind of past he would be able to share with someone when his time came to be in Hector's seat.

He suddenly realized that he knew nothing of Hector's son and his family. He knew nothing of how Hector had come to be in Pennsylvania, or how he had come to be at the gas station at two-thirty in the morning. For all that he knew about Hector from his stories, there was so much more that he didn't know, that he never would know.

Hector looked over at him and their eyes met for just a fraction of a second. Even in the dark, Jason was able to see the peace and caring in Hector's eyes.

That would be a good way to grow old, he thought, returning his eyes to the road.

"What I would like to do, I guess," he said slowly, "is just leave it all behind me. Just move on with my life and not let it bother me any more."

"Can you do that?" Hector asked.

"I don't know how."

Hector shifted in his seat. "I do not want to be a bother, but I would like to ask you if you can stop at the next exit so that I can use the bathroom. I drank a bit too much soda at dinner."

"Sure," Jason agreed. "I need to get gas, anyway."

"Thank you very much."

They didn't speak any more until they reached the next exit, where they could see from the road a large service station sign glowing brightly in the dark.

"I thank you for this," Hector said. "This definitely is an emergency." As the car came to a stop, he opened the door and practically leaped out, walking quickly to the door of the station. Jason smiled as he got out of the car and started to pump the gas. He never would have guessed that Hector would have so much spryness in him. He watched through the windows as Hector made his way to the back of the store where the restrooms were.

He sighed as he watched the pump's display run up the numbers of both the gallons pumped and the price that was going to be charged to his credit card. He wasn't sure why he was sighing—it just felt right. He had known Hector less than twenty-four hours now, and he already felt that he was able to tell him many more things than he had told anyone else in years. Somehow he felt like he had lucked into gaining a grandfather for a day or two, and he was able for the first time in his life to hear the wise advice that a grandfather might give him. He was able to share the experiences of someone who had been on the planet much longer than him, and who was willing to listen, not just talk. He felt a certain relief being able to talk with someone who not only cared for him just because he was who he was, but who had no preconceived expectations of him.

Perhaps the sigh had come because he had never met either of his grandfathers. Perhaps it was because he knew that he would have to drop Hector off in Pocatello sometime fairly soon. Or maybe he had sighed because even though he liked to hear what Hector said, he wasn't a bit sure that he would be able to use it to make the slightest bit of difference in his life.

When the gas pump clicked off, he put the nozzle back in its slot and took his receipt. Hector was just coming out of the store then, walking more calmly and singing a song softly to himself.

"I'm gonna go in and use the bathroom myself and get some coffee," Jason said. "I'll be right back."

"That is fine," Hector said. "I will clean off the windshield while I wait."

"Oh, thanks," Jason said, surprised that he had forgotten to do so. He had been wanting to clean it since dinner, yet somehow it had slipped his mind. "I'll be right back."

"You take your time," Hector said. "The road is very patient—it will wait for us as long as we need."

Jason smiled. "Someday I hope to be as full of wise sayings as you are, Hector," he called out as he walked away. He entered the store and started towards the restroom when the attendant called out to him.

"Excuse me," he said, "but is that your grandfather who was just in here?" The man was in his late twenties, with long blond hair and a look that said that he didn't have much patience with anyone, at least not that night. He was scowling, and Jason wondered why.

"No, he's not related to me," he replied, walking over to the counter. "I'm just giving him a ride. Why? What's up?"

"He stole some cookies, that's what's up." His voice was exasperated, impatient, but not unkind. "I need someone to pay for them, or I'm gonna have to call the cops. Store policy."

"No, no—don't do that. I'll pay for them. Just let me go to the bathroom, okay? I've got to get some coffee anyway, and I'll pay for them then." He looked out the window to where Hector was cleaning the windows of his car. "I'm sorry about that—I'm really sorry."

"Well hey, it's not your fault. It's just that someone has to pay for them. I really don't want to have to call the cops." With Jason's promise of payment, the edge has left his voice.

"I'll be right back," Jason promised. As he walked to the bathroom, he suddenly was afraid of what might be happening to Hector. Why had he stolen cookies? What was going on in his mind? Was he losing touch with reality once more? And if he was, what was Jason going to do about it?

After he finished in the bathroom, he got his coffee and a donut and returned to the register.

"It was one of these," the attendant said, holding up a four-pack of cookies. "He just grabbed them as he walked by and put them into his shirt pocket. I was going to follow him out and get them back when I saw you come in. I figured it would be easier for everyone if there wasn't any hassle, you know."

"Yes, I do know," Jason said. "And I appreciate it very much. And I'm really sorry he did that. I didn't have any reason to think he'd do something like this."

"Hey, it's cool," the attendant assured him, his voice now friendly and relaxed. "Happens all the time in here, you know. People just keep passing through, they think they're completely anonymous and no one's ever gonna find them on the highway. Most of the time it's just petty crap that it's not even worth calling the cops for. They get pretty pissed that I call them here because someone swiped a candy bar or a pack of condoms, you know."

"Yeah, I can imagine," Jason said. "Seems like they'd have better things to do with their time, huh?"

"You got it. So the company just writes it all off and charges you more for your coffee to make up for the thieves. Next time you see someone who shoplifts, you should tell him 'You're welcome,' because you pay for all the shit he steals."

Jason put his change in his pocket and picked up his stuff. "Thanks for your understanding," he said. "Have a good night."

Everybody has their story to tell, he thought as he walked to the door, wondering what he was going to say to Hector. He looked at his car and saw that Hector was already in the front seat, sitting quietly and waiting for him.

The windshield was spotless, and Jason got in the car and got settled, not sure what to say to Hector.

"I've cleaned the windshield," Hector said with pride in his voice. "I also did all of the windows. They're very clean now."

Jason looked carefully at him—his voice sounded different, not nearly as confident and wise as it had sounded before. It sounded almost childlike in it inflections. Hector looked back at him with a small smile on his face, and a gleam in his eyes. Jason didn't feel that he was looking at the same man.

"Oh, shit," he muttered.

"Do you like the windows?" Hector asked.

Jason quickly looked at the windshield, then back at Hector. He didn't think it was the right moment to bring up the cookies. "Of course I like them," he replied. "They look great. You did a great job."

"I did them all myself," Hector said.

"Yes, you did, Hector," Jason said quietly, turning on the car engine.

Chapter Ten

He drove out of the station and back on the highway without another word. Until they reached the highway, Hector sat quietly by his side. Jason was stunned at the change in Hector, confused by the different person who sat there next to him. What had happened? Had Hector forgotten to take some sort of medication? Did he have Alzheimer's? He obviously wasn't faking, but what was going on? If Hector had 'lost his mind,' how long would it take him to get it back?

Suddenly Hector started talking to himself very quietly in Spanish. Jason looked over at him; he was staring straight ahead at the road, sitting very low in his seat with his arms crossed before him, each hand grasping the other elbow. Jason had no idea of what he might be saying, and Hector's intonation gave away nothing as to what the words might mean. His tone was conversational, and there was no anger or anguish or sadness or elation in the sound of his voice.

"Hey, Hector," Jason said, "Are you in there somewhere?"

Hector continued talking, as if he hadn't heard Jason speak.

"Oh, great," Jason muttered. What am I supposed to do now? he asked himself. He didn't seem to have too many options. Pocatello was still more than twenty-four hours away, not including sleep. That put him in the car for more than thirty hours with this new Hector, this person that he didn't know and didn't understand.

And what was he supposed to do once he reached Pocatello? Look up Hector's relatives? Try to find someone who could take care of him? Or should he just drop him off at the police station? Or would a hospital be better? He had no idea what he should do. He certainly couldn't just leave him at a gas station in this condition. Life had just complicated itself significantly, and he didn't have any answers as to how he could un-complicate things.

"I guess we'll just have to cross those bridges when we come to them, Hector," he said aloud, looking over at his passenger once more. Hector gave no sign that he had heard. "This is gonna make one hell of a story when I have someone to tell it to," Jason said. Then he reached out and turned on the radio for the first time in many hours, at a very low volume.

The next few hours were difficult. Jason tried to turn up the music several times when songs that he liked came on, trying to give himself something else to listen to other than the drone of Hector's non-stop voice, but each time Hector reached out and turned the volume back down. Hector never looked at Jason any more—he always looked straight out the windshield in front of him or down at the floor. Jason tried to talk to him several times, but he never got any response. Jason was thankful that at least Hector wasn't talking loudly.

Being in his car had changed. Thirty-six hours ago, his car had represented his freedom, his independence, his journey to a new life, and it was his. Sitting behind the wheel had given him the power to choose his own destination, his own destiny. When he had taken on Hector as a passenger, his car was no longer his alone, and it offered him no solitude, no independence. But it still offered him a pleasant place to be, especially after he and Hector had started getting along well together. He actually had started to look forward to getting back in the car for their conversations after they stopped for gas or food. Hector seemed a kindred soul in many ways, and Jason had come to appreciate his stories and his insights.

Now, though, the experience was different. He was now nervous about this person in the seat next to him, just inches away from him. This wasn't the Hector that he had come to know and to trust. This was some other person, someone with whom he couldn't communicate, someone who for all he knew might be unstable and untrustworthy.

He found himself feeling resentment towards this new Hector. In his mind he started to see him as someone who had taken away the other Hector. Somehow, it was this guy's fault that the other Hector wasn't there any more. That's ridiculous, he told himself—this guy didn't have anything to do with that. Hell, this is Hector. He's just changed.

He found that his focus had changed. Instead of hearing Hector's stories and even telling him about something of his own past, Jason's mind now was constantly on what he would do when he reached Pocatello. He decided that he would have to take Hector to a hospital, but what would happen if they wouldn't take him? And how was he going to explain things there? Would they believe him?

"Hi there. I hope I'm in the right place, because I don't know what to do with this man here. He asked me for a ride to Pocatello in Pennsylvania a couple of days ago, and he's been riding with me since. Night before last he changed, though—before that he was pretty normal, but since then all he's been doing is sitting there, talking to himself. He doesn't respond to anything at all, and I really have no idea what I'm supposed to be doing with him."

He rehearsed speeches like that over and over, but nothing satisfied him. He thought of all the possible outcomes—what would he do if they were to give him the address of someplace else to take him? What if they wouldn't take him at all? "I'm sorry, sir, but we're not equipped to handle vagrants who don't seem to have any medical emergency." Would a hospital take him if there were obviously nothing wrong with him physically? And what would he do if they wouldn't? Then he'd have to leave Hector in the parking lot, because there definitely was nothing else that he possibly could do for him.

Hector didn't deserve that kind of treatment, though.

By the time he had to pull over to sleep, he had gone through all the scenarios he possibly could think of for taking Hector to the hospital in the morning. As he entered the rest area, a new problem entered his mind—did he really want to go to sleep with this new Hector right next to him? Did he really have a choice? There was no way he could go on driving all night. Maybe he should find a hotel and rent two rooms? Rent one room and leave Hector out in the car? It didn't seem that Hector would mind much of anything in his current state.

And just then he thought of another problem: was Hector able to use the bathroom in this state? Was he potty-trained? He didn't even want to start thinking about the possible problems that would come up if he weren't able to get Hector to use the bathroom.

"Damn it, Hector," he said aloud, the first words he had said in at least an hour, "you sure have complicated my life for me, haven't you?"

Hector didn't reply.

Jason parked at the far end of the lot once more. "I'm going to the bathroom," he said to Hector. "Do you need to go, too?" Hector didn't respond, didn't look at him. "Bathroom?" Jason tried again. "Do you need to go to the bathroom?"

He got out of the car and opened Hector's door for him. "Let's go to the bathroom, Hector," he said quietly, patiently. "We've got to use the bathroom." He reached down and gently took Hector by the arm. At the touch, Hector looked up at him for the first time, and in the light of the streetlamps Jason saw the child in his glance, the trusting neediness of a very young person. Hector allowed himself to be pulled from the car, then allowed Jason to lead him to the bathrooms. He stopped talking as they walked, shuffling his feet much more than he had before. He seemed to be uncomfortable with walking, as if he were afraid of what he would find if he kept on going.

"Oh, Hector," Jason said sadly, quietly. "What's happened to you? Are you still in there? Are you trying to get out?"

Hector didn't answer—he just continued shuffling onwards as silently as he had sat when he had first got in the car.

Jason was relieved that Hector knew exactly what a toilet was for and that he knew how to use one without help. Sooner than he had hoped they were back at the car. Jason hoped that Hector would be able to go to sleep instead of sitting there talking to himself. Otherwise, he didn't think that he'd be getting much sleep himself. In any case, he should be able to rest a lot, even if he didn't sleep.

He reclined his seat and lay his head back, looking over at Hector, who sat quietly with his eyes closed, breathing heavily. He seemed to have gotten the idea about sleep, for he seemed to be fast asleep almost immediately.

What was going on in his mind? Jason asked himself. How could someone as wise and coherent as Hector have suddenly lost his ability to think and to share his thoughts? Was that Hector still in there, somehow trapped and unable to come out, to express himself and share of himself? And if he was trapped in there, was he aware that he was trapped? It seemed to Jason that it must be hell to be trapped in a body, in a mind, that wouldn't allow him to be himself.

He closed his eyes and relaxed as much as he could. He didn't expect to sleep deeply because of all that was going on in his mind and all the inertia that his body had been experiencing. Almost as soon as he closed his eyes, though, the image of the little girl in the wrecked van came to mind, and he had to look at her pleading eyes in his memory once more. He couldn't handle it, so he opened his eyes immediately.

"Great," he mumbled sleepily, looking over at Hector once more. He turned his head and body so that he was facing his window, and he watched the taillights of the cars out on the Interstate for several minutes until he dozed off.

When he awoke, he had no idea where he was. It was still dark, and it took him several long moments to get his bearings. Once he realized he was in his car, the rest came quickly. He turned around and looked at Hector, who was still sleeping, and he pushed the button on the stereo that illuminated the clock. 4:20. It wouldn't be long until the sun came up. He had slept longer than he thought he would, but he wasn't too worried about that—a little bit of extra sleep would come in handy and keep him on the road longer.

He started the car and slowly pulled out of the rest area, debating whether or not he should wake up Hector and make him use the bathroom again. He decided to leave well enough alone—he'd deal with Hector when Hector woke up. There was no reason to do so before that.

Hector slept another two hours, and by the time he woke up Jason was pretty desperate to use the bathroom himself. He half-hoped that Hector somehow would wake up as he was before, able to talk and listen and give wise advice. When he awoke, though, he said nothing—Jason wouldn't even have known that he was awake if he hadn't looked over and seen his eyes staring straight ahead once more.

Jason sighed. "Good morning, Hector," he said, but there was no response. He reached out and touched Hector softly on the arm, and then Hector looked over at him. "Good morning, Hector," Jason repeated, and Hector smiled. Jason put his hand back on the steering wheel, and Hector turned his head to look forward once more.

Jason took the next exit that had a gas station, and he walked Hector inside to the bathroom before he pumped gas. He didn't want an incident like the one in the last place. The attendant looked at them a bit oddly as he led Hector to the door, but Jason didn't care at that point. He knew what he had to do, and he knew that this man had no idea of what was truly going on, so what he thought or how he looked really didn't matter at all.

Hector went inside the bathroom, and Jason poured himself a cup of coffee while he waited. Then he picked up a small pack of donuts for them to split. They had a long day of driving ahead of them, and he hoped that the donuts would be enough to tide them over until lunch. He took them to the register just as the bathroom door opened.

"I'll be right back," Jason told the attendant. "I'm just going to put him in the car."

The cashier raised his eyebrows, but he didn't say a word. He looked groggy, and Jason was sure that he was finishing up the night shift.

He led Hector outside and put him into the car, reaching in and buckling his seatbelt for him and closing the door. He hoped that Hector would stay there and not go wandering off like some people with Alzheimer's that he had read about from time to time. Then he went back inside and used the bathroom himself, grabbed a bottle of orange juice for Hector, just in case, then paid for the coffee and donuts.

"Is that it?" the attendant asked.

"Yeah, that's it. Thanks."

"Is that your grandpa?"

Jason smiled. "Sort of—it's a long story. I guess you could call him my adopted grandfather."

"It looks like he's pretty much out of it, doesn't it?"

"I guess that would be one way of putting it," Jason said. "He seems to be pretty much out of everything, at the moment, unfortunately."

"Must be rough," the cashier said, giving Jason his change. "My grandma kind of went that way. She lost everything, you know? No memory, she didn't recognize anyone, couldn't have a conversation with her. I didn't get the feeling that it was all that hard on her, but I don't know. I could have been wrong, I guess."

"Yeah, it's hard to tell. I have no idea if this is hard on him, or if it's just hard on me."

"Well, you have a good day. And a good trip."

"Thank you, I will. You, too. The day part, not the trip part."

The attendant laughed. "You got that right—I sure ain't going anywhere. No trips for me."

Jason put everything on the top of the car when he reached it, pulled out his credit card, and started pumping gas. This was probably his next-to-last gas stop before Pocatello, and that was a bit of a relief to him—he wanted the whole drama to end somehow, and preferably soon. It was one thing to offer a ride to someone, but quite another to end up babysitting someone he wasn't qualified to take care of.

He watched Hector as he filled the tank with gas. He still sat quietly, not moving a bit, looking straight ahead. That was sad to Jason, who remembered how much Hector had looked around, how he seemed to catch every detail with his intelligent, knowing eyes. Now he seemed to catch nothing, comprehend nothing.

When he finished with the gas, Jason simply didn't want to get in the car again. He fought the urge to go inside and ask the attendant if there was a hospital in the area where he could leave Hector. He knew he couldn't live with himself knowing that he was so close to getting Hector home, only to drop him off with strangers short of his destination. He took a deep breath, then released it slowly. Then he picked up the coffee, donuts, and orange juice and got into the car with Hector.

"Are you all ready to go home, Hector?" he asked, trying to sound cheerful. "We've got one more day, and then you'll be there." There was no response.

On the highway again, Jason felt tears start to form in his eyes, and he blinked quickly to try to stop them, then he dried his eyes with his sleeve. The last thing he needed now was to break down crying. He wasn't even sure what he was crying about, either—was it Hector, or the little girl? Or was it her family, or the truck driver who was still in his seat with the staring, unseeing eyes? Or was it maybe the people he had left behind, or the fear of the unknown place he was going to? Or was it simply the fact that things were piling up faster than he could deal with them, faster than he could even keep track of all that was going on.

"I miss you, Hector," he said quietly, hoping against hope that he might be able to reach the man who had to be in there somewhere.

Hector gave no response still. Jason opened the pack of donuts and held one out to Hector, who didn't even seem to notice it. Jason sighed and put the donut on a napkin on the dashboard in front of Hector in case he got the urge to eat. Then he pulled out a donut for himself and ate it slowly, doing his best to taste every bite fully, washing each bite down with a sip of coffee. Coffee and donuts were his favorite food combination of all, and he had a sudden urge to make sure that he noticed and felt everything that he could at that moment. That's how Hector would have done it, he told himself. Maybe I can take some lessons from the man that Hector was up until last night.

He did his best to watch the trees in the early morning light as they went by outside the car, to see the sky above them, to appreciate the mountains that now stood watch in the far distance. He kept replaying Hector's words and ideas in his mind, but they were already getting mixed up and fuzzy. Jason couldn't be sure that any of the words in his memory were the actual words that he had heard, or perhaps just what he had wanted to hear, or how he preferred to remember them. He knew the gist of the ideas, though, and he had to be happy with that. There wasn't much left other than that.

"You know what, Hector?" he suddenly asked aloud. "I know that you're in there somewhere. Maybe it's time that I paid you back for all the stories you told me. Maybe it's my turn to tell you some of my stories. Would you want to hear some of my stories?" He turned and looked at Hector, then looked back at the road.

"Well, you should be a good listener, anyway. It doesn't look like you'll do a whole lot of interrupting." He settled in his seat a bit and got more comfortable. "I never told you about the time that my brother and I found all those snakes, did I? I couldn't have, because it just came back to me." And he told Hector the story of finding the snakes and trying to catch them, and how he had killed one accidentally, and how he had felt when he realized that the snake was dead at his hand.

And when that story was done, he told Hector all about the time he and some friends had almost been arrested while he was in college, and he told about his first date with a girl his junior year in high school, how awkward and unnatural he had felt. He told him how he had met Lance, and he told him the story of when he had finally admitted to himself that he was gay, and how it felt when he finally stopped fighting the idea and trying to fit himself into a way of being that felt so unreal to him.

When he finished a story, he rested, watching the road fly by, watching the towns go by, watching the numbers on the mileage signs go down until they passed a place, then go up when a new city's name appeared. He thought of new stories to tell, and he tried to think of new ways to tell them. He stopped for lunch and bought nothing but chicken nuggets that he could feed to Hector one by one, without any sauce. He made bathroom stops and late in the afternoon he made another gas stop, one that he thought would be his last one before Pocatello. From time to time he would reach out and turn up the radio to see if Hector's reflexes were still okay, and each time Hector reached out immediately and turned it down.

He spent some time wondering what kinds of stories Hector might be telling if he still were able to do so. Would he learn why Hector had been in Pennsylvania? Would he learn about Hector's son?

He noticed the cycles of the road more strongly than he had before—drive, eat, drive, sleep, drive, eat. He noticed how normal it all had become to him, how quickly it had become his reality, displacing the cycles that he had been living up until two days ago.

The morning passed, then the afternoon. As he drove through the late-night darkness, he couldn't help but remember just how important the darkness had been to him so recently, and just how unimportant it was to him now. He didn't need it any more, didn't need its isolation, its comfort. He saw its comfort now as a false promise, a warped idea of insulation and independence.

He woke up the next morning about an hour and a half east of Ogden, and as he led Hector to the bathroom he knew that the end was getting near, that he would have to leave Hector. It would be painful to leave him in this condition, painful to leave him without a good-bye, but there really was no choice. He had no words to say as he led Hector back to the car and headed back out onto the highway.

He was more tired than he ever remembered being, and he had a feeling that he might have to stop soon and sleep again. It scared him to be on the road when he was sleepy. But he also had to do something with Hector, and he was torn between wanting to get it over with as quickly as possible and wanting to delay the moment of their parting as much as he could.

He had just reached up to flip down his rear-view mirror to hide the rising sun behind him when he saw Hector looking about himself for the first time in almost thirty-six hours.

"Hector?" he asked, his voice full of hope.

Hector looked at him. "Good morning, Jason," he said quietly.

"Hey, you're back!" Jason exclaimed, elated. "It's been a while, amigo."

Hector slowly buried his face in his hands for several long moments, then looked up again.

"I have been gone?" he asked.

Suddenly Jason was sad to see the way Hector felt. He was glad to have him back, but he knew that "going away" wasn't something pleasant for Hector. "Yeah," he sighed. "You've been gone for almost a day and a half. Do you remember any of it?"

Hector shook his head. "I remember nothing. Nothing at all. Not of that time. I remember the time before that, but nothing since we stopped for gas at night."

"Yeah, that's pretty much when you checked out. We're just a few hours away from Pocatello, now."

"Then I hope that I will be able to say good-bye to my son and his family. I was very afraid that I would not be able to. This time, it was very short. There have been times that I have been gone for weeks. I am very afraid that one day I will go and not come back, but my body will live on without my spirit. That is no life, and eventually I would die without being able to say good-bye to this world that has given so much to me. I wish to leave on my own terms, with my own mind still functioning."

Jason sat quietly. He could hear the distress in Hector's voice, and he couldn't even imagine what it must feel like to have his mind go away so completely like that.

"I do not wish to hold on to life simply to keep my heart beating as long as possible. It makes no sense if it is not me in the body, but just a body existing without spirit. Much of our desire to hold on to life comes from our fear of leaving others alone and a fear of what might await us when we pass on to whatever comes next. I have no fear of either."

"What do you mean?" Jason asked, growing suspicious. "You aren't going to kill yourself, are you?"

Hector shrugged.

Jason didn't know what to say, so he said nothing. They drove on in silence for a very long time, and soon they were heading north instead of east, soon they were within a couple of hours of Pocatello. Hector seemed content to sit there silently, so Jason remained silent. He turned the radio up slightly, and Hector didn't reach out to turn it down.

Jason was glad to have Hector back, but the silence was disturbing. There was something very final about it, something disconcerting. He had gotten used to Hector not saying anything over the last day and a half, but that had been a different Hector. Now that the original Hector was back, the Hector that recognized him and that could talk and listen and understand, why wasn't he talking? Why was he staying so quiet?

He was relieved that he wouldn't have to make decisions about what to do with Hector now, but everything was growing far larger than he was prepared to deal with. Here he had given a ride to a man who had become a friend to him, almost a member of his family in an odd sort of way, yet who had disappeared from sight behind the empty eyes of a different man. For a long time, his voice had been gone, his ideas had left, his friendliness and wisdom had disappeared. Now he was back, but he wasn't. Hector was different now, and Jason didn't know what would be expected of him now.

On top of Hector's disappearance and reappearance he had the little girl's eyes still with him, still clear in his mind. What had that look demanded of him, and had he come through in the way he was supposed to? Or should he have given something else other than the slight effort it had taken him to get someone else to deal with her? Add those things to the uncertainty of his near future and the uncertainty that he even had a long-term future to look forward to, and all of a sudden Jason felt completely overwhelmed, as if he had been given five years worth of life to live in and had had it all crammed into just over 72 hours. And there seemed to be no one there any longer to share the burden with, no one with whom he could talk things over. Hector had been there as a friendly ear, someone with whom he could share ideas and thoughts, but now Hector no longer seemed to be that kind of person.

The last two hours dragged by very slowly in awkward silence. Finally, as they approached the southern end of Pocatello, Hector spoke once more.

"They will be buried in the Mountain View Cemetery," he said quietly. "They will be next to Leigh, just as I will be. I will tell you how to get there."

"Okay, *amigo*," Jason said. "You give me directions, and I'll get you there."

And he did. They arrived at the cemetery in the mid-morning of a beautiful day. The sun was shining brightly and the temperature was in the mid-70's. As they stepped out of Jason's car, a cool breeze greeted them.

"It is a beautiful day," Hector remarked, looking up at the sky and stretching his arms. "If Leigh were with me on this day, we most certainly would go for a very long walk to enjoy the sunshine and the breeze."

"It is nice," Jason agreed, looking around at the headstones that surrounded them, at the mountains that looked over the scene, at the trees that were scattered about. It was the flattest cemetery that Jason had ever seen, much different than the rolling, tree-filled New England cemeteries that he was used to. There was a certain charm to the openness, a certain feeling of freedom and openness. Compared to this place, the cemeteries in his memory seemed claustrophobic.

He followed Hector, who was walking with determination towards a certain spot.

"Here she is," he said when he found Leigh's grave. He reached out and gently touched the writing on the stone, the letters of her name. "Her body has been here for quite a while, but I do not know exactly where her spirit is. I will find out soon enough, I am sure."

He looked at the stone to the right of Leigh's, where three names were written: Timothy Gutierrez, Laneya Gutierrez, and Monica Gutierrez. He stepped over in front of the headstone and dropped to his knees, bowing his head. Jason saw tears in his eyes. Hector stayed like that for a full minute before he raised his head. His cheeks were streaked with tears that Hector made no effort to wipe away.

"Timothy was a very interesting child," he said. "As a child he was the most contrary person I ever knew. We could say nothing that he did not argue with, nothing that did not cause some sort of conflict with him. This trait continued as he grew up. There were many times that I felt that he was being argumentative because he did not like me or respect me, and I sometimes even thought that he disliked me or even hated me. Leigh was very good at reminding me that the conflict was not about who I was, but about who Timothy was and how he saw the world and related to it. It was often very hard for me to believe her when she told me this, but I did my best.

"I never believed that Timothy would succeed in life. It must sound awful for a father to say such a thing about his son. I thought always that he would be too difficult for people to deal with, that he would not respect other people's ideas or opinions. I was very skeptical when he announced that he wished to become a doctor, for I did not believe that his demeanor would serve him well when working with patients. I was proved to be very wrong, though. Timothy was an excellent doctor. It is hard to believe that he is no longer in this world with us. The world will miss him."

"'Any man's death diminishes me, because I am involved in mankind.'"

"John Donne. That is a beautiful poem. I am very impressed that you know it. Timothy worked with children, which suited him very well because he probably would have had a hard time working with adult patients. Look, his grave is covered with flowers—I suppose from people that he treated and cared for. And probably from Laneya's family. I do not know. They are beautiful flowers, though."

Hector turned to Jason. "Could you please get my bag from the car, Jason? There is something in there that I would like you to have."

"Uh, sure." Jason was surprised. Hector's words had interested him, but he was wondering where they would go from there, where he would take Hector. He went back to the car and took Hector's small blue bag from the floor of the passenger side. As he turned back towards Hector, he saw him put something in his mouth, then take a drink of water.

A sudden sense of dread washed over him, and he fought the urge to run back to the graveside. He did walk quickly.

"Um, Hector—what did you just put in your mouth?" he asked cautiously. Hector didn't respond. "Please tell me that you didn't just do what I think you did."

Hector smiled, then walked the few steps to Leigh's grave. "It is a beautiful day, is it not?" he asked, putting his hand upon her headstone.

"Hector, what did you just take? What did you just do?"

Hector looked at him carefully, and Jason was amazed at the peace in Hector's face. "I believe that you know what I just did, Jason. I feel fortunate that I am able to be at this place with a person I care about very much on such a beautiful morning. I truly have been blessed by my circumstances."

"Hector, you can't do this. Look, you need to walk around, keep on your feet. I'll go find someone with a cell phone and call an ambulance for you."

"No, Jason, you will not."

Hector's voice made Jason stop in his tracks. He knew that Hector was right.

"This is my choice, Jason. I do not wish to finish my life as the person who was in the car with you for so long yesterday. I remember nothing of that time, and I do not want to finish my life with no memories, no thoughts of beauty, no gratitude, no love, no feelings."

"Hector, you can't just—" Jason stopped as Hector held up his right hand, palm toward Jason.

"Jason, I have an opportunity here to die a beautiful death. Please do not ruin it by trying to change it to fit your vision of how things should be. It is the only chance I will get to do it well."

Jason stared into Hector's eyes, then his shoulders dropped as the tension left his body. He exhaled loudly, as if he had just accepted the unacceptable.

"Could you please give me my bag?" Jason stepped over to Hector and handed him the bag. Hector reached into an outside pocket and pulled something out. He held it out to Jason, a small refrigerator magnet. Jason took it and turned it over, and he saw a poorly made four-color rainbow. He smiled.

"The quality is not so good. But that truly does not matter." Hector sat down on the ground, his back against Leigh's tombstone.

"No, it doesn't," Jason said, fighting his tears. "I'll miss you, Hector."

"Of course you will," Hector said with a smile. "Friends always miss friends. I thank you with all my heart for bringing me to this place."

"It's nothing." Jason's voice was weak. He walked over to Hector, and he sat down on the ground next to him.

"Crying is very good," Hector said, a tear sliding down his own face. "I will miss this world and all its beauty. Please remember to see it."

"I will." They sat in silence for a few moments, and Jason could actually feel Hector growing weaker next to him. "Hey, Hector?"

"Yes?" Hector replied, his voice already distant and weak.

"How do you say 'grandfather' in Spanish?"

"*Abuelo.*"

"How do you say 'my grandfather'?"

"*Mi abuelo.*'"

Jason put his arm around Hector's shoulder and felt the frailness of the old man's body. "I love you, *mi abuelo.*"

"I love you, too, *mijo*," Hector said so softly that Jason almost didn't hear him. Then he lay his head on Jason's shoulder and closed his eyes.

About the Author

Tom Walsh was born quite a few years ago in Long Beach, California. Growing up in a Navy family, he would end up living in San Francisco, San Diego, Norfolk, Virginia Beach, Great Lakes, IL and Tucson and Safford, AZ before he graduated from high school in Safford. He then went on to the University of Arizona, where he graduated with a B.A. in Spanish.

From there, he went to live in Barcelona and Salamanca, Spain; Munich, Germany; and then back to Barcelona, staying three years in Europe. He came back to the states to study Teaching English as a Second Language, earning an M.A. from Northern Arizona University before going into the U.S. Army as a linguist/intelligence analyst. He spent four years in the service, studying at the Defense Language Institute's Russian program and serving in Augsburg, Germany for over two years as a German and Russian linguist.

He returned to the states again to study at the University of Northern Colorado, where he earned M.A.'s in English and Educational Leadership and Policy Studies. After finishing those programs, he moved to New Hampshire, where he taught at St. Anselm College and various other schools as adjunct faculty before starting with Landmark College in Putney, VT, a college designed to teach only students with Learning Disabilities.

In 2005, he earned his Ph.D. in Teaching and Learning from Capella University.

His hobbies are reading, writing, maintaining his website (livinglifefully.com), listening to music, going for walks, photography, and trying to keep his parts of the house uncluttered (a usually-hopeless task). He's married to Terry and has three step-children, Andy, Caryn, and Jess.

Also by Tom:

(If I Should Die) Before I Wake (available from Amazon.com)